Phebe Earle Gibbons

Pennsylvania Dutch

and Other Essays

Phebe Earle Gibbons

Pennsylvania Dutch
and Other Essays

ISBN/EAN: 9783337301149

Printed in Europe, USA, Canada, Australia, Japan

Cover: Foto ©Andreas Hilbeck / pixelio.de

More available books at **www.hansebooks.com**

"PENNSYLVANIA DUTCH,"

AND

OTHER ESSAYS.

"Along the cool sequestered vale of life
They kept the noiseless tenor of their way."

PHILADELPHIA:
J. B. LIPPINCOTT & CO.
1872.

THE leading article in this collection was written about four years ago, and appeared in the *Atlantic Monthly* for 1869.

In publishing it now, I make a few alterations and add notes.

After this was written, I became better acquainted with our plain German sects, and wrote the other essays that describe them, and which are graver, and more strictly historical, than the first.   G.

APRIL, 1872.

CONTENTS.

	PAGE
"Pennsylvania Dutch" (properly German) . .	9
Language	9
Religion	12
History of the Sect	20
Politics	22
Festivals	24
Weddings	26
Quiltings	33
Farming	35
Farmers' Wives	39
Holidays	49
Public Schools	53
Manners and Customs	56
An Amish Meeting	60
Swiss Exiles	73
The Dunker Love-Feast	109
Ephrata	139
A Friend	178
Cousin Jemima	198

"PENNSYLVANIA DUTCH"

(PROPERLY GERMAN).

I HAVE lived for twenty years in the county of Lancaster, where my neighbors on all sides are "Pennsylvania Dutch." In this article, I shall try to give, from my own observation and familiar acquaintance, some account of the life of a people who are almost unknown outside of the rural neighborhoods of their own State, who have much that is peculiar in their language, customs, and beliefs, and whom I have learned heartily to esteem for their native good sense, friendly feeling, and religious character.

LANGUAGE.

The tongue which these people speak is a dialect of the German, but they generally call it and themselves "Dutch."

For the native German who works with them on the farm they entertain some contempt, and the title "Yankee" is with them a syhonym for cheat.* As must always be the case where the great majority do not read the tongue which they speak, and live in contact with those who speak another, the language has become mixed and corrupt. Seeing a young neighbor cleaning a buggy, I tried to talk with him by speaking German. "Willst du reiten?" said I (not remembering that *reiten* is to ride on horseback). "Willst du reiten?" All my efforts were vain. I was going for cider to the house of a neighboring farmer, and there I asked his daughter what she would say, under the circumstances, for "Are you going to ride?"

"Widdu fawry? Buggy fawry?" was the answer. (Willst du fahren?) Such expressions are heard as "Koockamulto'," for "Guck einmal da," or "Just look at that!" and "Haltybissel" for "Halt ein biszchen," or "Wait a little bit." "Gutenobit" is used for "Guten Abend." Apple-butter is "Lodwaerrick," from the German "Latwerge," an electuary, or an electuary of

---

* An acquaintance explains the prejudice against Yankees, by telling how, some forty to sixty years ago, the tin-peddlers traveled among the innocent Dutch people, cheating the farmers and troubling the daughters. They were (says he) tricky, smart, and good-looking. They could tell a good yarn, and were very amusing, and the goodly hospitable farmers would take them into their houses and entertain them, and receive a little tin-ware in payment.

prunes. Our "Dutch" is much mixed with English. I once asked a woman what pie-crust is in Dutch. "Py-kroosht," she answered.

Those who speak English use uncommon expressions, as,—"That's a werry *lasty* basket" (meaning durable); "I seen him yet a'ready;" "I knew a woman that had a good baby *wunst;*" "The bread is all" (all gone). I have heard the carpenter call his plane *she*, and a housekeeper apply the same pronoun to her home-made soap.

A rich landed proprietor is sometimes called *king*. An old "Dutchman" who was absent from home thus narrated the cause of his journey: "I must go and see old Yoke (Jacob) Beidelman. Te people calls me te kink ov te Manor (township), and tay calls him te kink ov te Octorara. Now, dese kinks must come togeder once." (Accent *together*, and pass quickly over *once*.)*

---

* The most elegant specimens of Pennsylvania German with which I have met, are the poems of the late Rev. Henry Harbaugh; but, as the English words introduced by Mr. H. have since been in general substituted by German, the poems are not a perfect specimen of the spoken language.

Mr. Harbaugh says, in his poem of Homesickness, or Heimweh,—

   "Wie gleich ich selle Babble-Beem !
     Sie schtehn wie Brieder dar ;
   Un uf'm Gippel—g'wiss ich leb !
     Hockt alleweil 'n Schtaar !
   'S Gippel biegt sich—guk, wie's gaunscht,
     'R hebt sich awer fescht ;

RELIGION.

I called recently on my friend and neighbor,
Jacob S., who is a thrifty farmer, of a good mind,

> Ich seh sei rothe Fliegle plehn
>   Wann er sei Feddere weseht;
> Will wette, dass sei Fraale hot
>   Uf sellem Baam'n Neseht."

How well I love those poplar-trees,
  That stand like brothers there,
And on the top, as sure's I live,
  A blackbird perches now.
The top is bending, how it swings!
  But still the bird holds fast.
How plain I saw his scarlet wings
  When he his feathers dressed!
I'll bet you on that very tree
  His wifie has a nest.

Miss Rachel Bahn, of York County, has written some verses
in the dialect. She says:

> "Well, anyhow, wann's Frueyohr kummt,
>   Bin ich gepleased first-rate;
> Die luft's so fair un agenehm,
>   Die rose so lieblich webt.
> Nau gehe mei gedanke nuf
>   Wu's immer Frueyohr is,
> Wu's keh feren 'ring gewe duth,
>   Wu's herrlich is gewiss."

Well, anyhow, when springtime comes,
  Then am I pleased first-rate;
So fair and soft the breezes blow,
  So lovely is the rose.
'Tis then my thoughts are raised on high,
  Where Spring forever blooms,
Where change can never more be felt,
  But glory shines around.

and a member of the old Mennist or Mennonite
Society. I once accompanied him and his pleas-

Mr. E. H. Rauch, of Lancaster, has written some humorous
letters under the title of Pit (Pete) Schwefflebrenner.

He accommodates himself to the great numbers of our
"Dutch" people, who do not read German, by writing the
dialect phonetically. He says:

"Der klea meant mer awer, sei net recht g'sund, for er
kreisht ols so greisel-heftiet orrick (arg) in der nacht. De
olt Lawbucksy behawpt er is was mer aw gewocksa heast, un
meant mer set braucha derforo. Se sawya es waer an olty
fraw drivva im Lodwaerrickshteddle de kennt's aw wocksa
ferdreiv mit warta, un aw so a g'schmeer . . was se
mocht mit gensfet. . . . . De fraw sawya se waer a
sivvaty shweshter un a dochter fun eam daer sei dawdy nee
net g'sea hut . . . un sell gebt eara yetzt de gewalt so
warta braucha fors aw wocksa tsu ferdrieva."

"The little one seems to me not to be quite well, for he
cries so dreadfully in the night. Old Mrs. Lawbucks main-
tains that he is what we call grown (enlargement of the liver),
and thinks that I should do something for it. She says that
there was an old woman in Applebutter-town who knew how
to drive away the growth with words, and who has, too, an
ointment that she makes with goose-fat. . . The woman
says that she was a seventh sister, and the daughter of one who
never saw his father . . . and that gives her now the
power to use words to drive away the growth."

Professor Haldeman, of the University of Pennsylvania,
says that Pennsylvania German is a fusion of the South German dialects, brought from the region of the upper Rhine, including Switzerland, with an infusion of English.

He adds that the perfect is used for the imperfect tense, as
in Swiss; so that for "ich sagte" (I said), we have "ich hab

ant wife to their religious meeting. The meeting-house is a low brick building, with neat
surroundings, and resembles a Friends' meeting-
house. The Mennists in many outward circumstances very much resemble the Society of Friends,
but do not, like some of the latter, hold that the
object of extreme veneration is the teaching of
the Holy Spirit in the secret stillness of the soul.

In the interior of the Mennist meeting a
Quaker-like plainness prevails. The men, with
broad-brimmed hats and simple dress, sit on
benches on one side of the house, and the
women, in plain caps and black sun-bonnets, are
ranged on the other. The services are almost
always conducted in "Dutch," and consist of ex-
hortation and prayer, and singing by the congregation. The singing is without previous training,
and is not musical. A pause of about five minutes is allowed for private prayer.

The preachers are not paid, and are chosen in
the following manner. When a vacancy occurs,
and a new appointment is required, several men
go into a small room, appointed for the purpose; and to them waiting, enter singly the
men and women, as many as choose, who tell
them the name of the person whom each prefers

---

ksaat," for "ich hatte" (I had), we have "ich hab kat."—
*From the Transactions of the American Philological Associa-
tion, 1869–70.*

should fill the vacancy. After this, an opportunity is given to any candidate to excuse himself from the service. Those who are not excused, if, for instance, six in number, are brought before six books. Each candidate takes up a book, and the one within whose book a lot is found, is the chosen minister.

I asked my friends, who gave me some of these details, whether it was claimed or believed that there is any especial guidance of the Divine Spirit in thus choosing a minister. From the reply, I did not learn that any such guidance is claimed, though they spoke of a man who *was led* to pass his hand over all the other books, and who selected the last one, but he did not get the lot after all. He was thought to be ambitious of a place in the ministry.

The three prominent sects of Mennonites all claim to be non-resistants, or *wehrlos.* The *old* Mennists, who are the most numerous and least rigid, vote at elections, and are allowed to hold such public offices as school director and road supervisor, but not to be members of the legislature. The ministers are expected not to vote. The members of this society cannot bring suit against any one; they can hold mortgages, but not judgment bonds. Like Quakers, they were not allowed to hold slaves, and they do not take oaths, nor deal in spirituous liquors.

My neighbor Jacob and I were once talking of

the general use of the word "Yankee" to denote one who is rather unfair in his dealings. They sometimes speak of a "Dutch Yankee;" and Jacob asked me whether, if going to sell a horse, I should tell the buyer every fault that I knew of the horse's having, as, he maintained, was the proper course. His brother-in-law, who was at times a horse-dealer, did not agree with him.

Titles do not abound among these plain neighbors of ours. Jacob's little son used to call him "Jake," as he heard the hired men do. Nevertheless, one of our New Mennist acquaintances was quite courtly in his address. This last-mentioned sect branched off some forty years ago, and claim to be *reformirt,* or to have returned to an older and more excellent standard. They do not vote at all. Their most striking peculiarity is this: if one of the members is disowned by the church, the other members of his own family who are members of the meeting are not allowed to eat at the same table with him, and his wife withdraws from him. A woman who worked in such a family told me how unpleasant it was to her to see that the father did not take his seat at the table, to which she was invited.

In support of this practice, they refer to the eleventh verse of the fifth chapter of First Corinthians: " But now I have written unto you not to keep company, if any man that is called a brother be a fornicator, or covetous, or an idolater, or a railer, or a drunkard, or an extortioner; with such an one *no not to eat.*" We have yet another sect among us, called Amish (pronounced Ommish). In former times these Mennists were sometimes known as "beardy men," but of late years the beard is not a distinguishing trait. It is said that a person once asked an Amish man the difference between themselves and another Mennist sect. "Vy, dey vears puttons, and ve vearsh hooks oont eyes;" and this is, in fact, a prime difference. All the Mennist sects retain the ordinances of baptism and the Lord's Supper, but most also practice feet-washing, and some sectarians "greet one another with a holy kiss."

On a Sunday morning Amish wagons, covered with yellow oil-cloth, may be seen moving toward the house of that member whose turn it is to have the meeting. Great have been the preparations there beforehand,—the whitewashing, the scrubbing, the polishing of tin and brass. Wooden benches and other seats are provided for the "meeting-folks," and the services resemble those already described. Of course, young mothers do not stay at home, but bring their infants with them. When the meeting is over, the congregation remain to dinner. Bean soup was formerly the principal dish on this occasion, but, with the progress of luxury, the farmers of a fat soil no longer confine themselves to so simple a diet. Imagine what a time of social intercourse this must be, transcending those hospitable gatherings, the quarterly meetings of Friends.

The Amish dress is peculiar; and the children are diminutive men and women. The women wear sun-bonnets and closely-fitting dresses, but often their figures look very trim, in brown, with green or other bright handkerchiefs meeting over the breast.

I saw a group of Amish at the railroad station the other day,—men, women, and a little boy. One of the young women wore a pasteboard sun-bonnet covered with black, and tied with narrow blue ribbon, among which showed the thick white strings of her Amish cap; a gray shawl, without fringe; a brown stuff dress, and a purple apron. One middle-aged man, inclined to corpulence, had coarse, brown, woolen clothes, and his pantaloons, without suspenders (in the Amish fashion), were unwilling to meet his waistcoat, and showed one or two inches of white shirt. No buttons were on his coat behind, but down the front were hooks and eyes. One young girl wore a bright-brown sun-bonnet, a green dress, and a light blue apron. The choicest figure, however, was the six-year-old, in a jacket, and with pantaloons plentifully plaited into the waistband behind; hair cut straight over the forehead, and hanging to the shoulders; and a round-crowned black wool hat, with an astoundingly wide brim. The little girls, down to two years old, wear the plain cap, and the handkerchief crossed upon the breast.

In Amish houses, the love of ornament appears in brightly scoured utensils,—how the brass ladles are made to shine !—and in embroidered towels, one end of the towel showing a quantity of work in colored cottons. When steel or elliptic springs were introduced, so great a novelty was not at first patronized by members of the meeting; but an infirm brother, desiring to visit his friends, directed the blacksmith to put a spring inside his wagon, under the seat, and since that time steel springs have become common. I have even seen a youth with flowing hair (as is common among the Mennists), and two trim-bodied damsels, riding in a very plain, uncovered buggy.

A. Z. rode in a common buggy; but he became a great backslider, poor man !

. It was an Amish man, not well versed in the English language, from whom I bought poultry, who sent me a bill for " chighans."

In mentioning some ludicrous circumstances, far be it from me to ignore the virtues of these primitive people.

HISTORY OF THE SECT.

The Mennonites are named from Simon Menno, a reformer, who died in 1561, though it is doubtful whether Menno founded the. sect. "The prevailing opinion among church historians, especially those of Holland, is that the origin of the Dutch Baptists may be traced to the Waldenses, and that Menno merely organized the concealed and scattered congregations as a denomination."*

The freedom of religious opinion which was allowed in Pennsylvania may have had the effect of drawing hither the Continental Europeans, who established themselves in the fertile lands of the western part of the county of Chester, now Lancaster. It was not until the revolution of 1848 that the different German states granted full civil rights to the Mennonites. In some cases this freedom has since been withdrawn. Hanover, in 1858, annulled the election of a representative to the second chamber, because he was a Mennonite. Much of this opposition probably is caused by the sect's refusing to take oaths.

---

* New American Cyclopædia. I have not yet found (1872) any distinct historical connection between the Waldenses and Mennonites, or Anabaptists. The Martyr-book ("Martyr's Mirror") endeavors to prove identity of doctrine, in opposition to infant baptism, to war, and to oaths.

Under those opposing circumstances in the Old World, it is not remarkable that the number of Mennonites in the United States is reported to exceed that in all the rest of the world put together. The Amish are named from Jacob Amen, a Swiss Mennonite preacher of the seventeenth century.

As I understand the Mennonites, they endeavor in church government literally to carry out the injunction of Jesus, " Moreover, if thy brother shall trespass against thee, go and tell him his fault between thee and him alone; if he shall hear thee, thou hast gained thy brother. But if he will not hear thee, then take with thee one or two more, that in the mouth of two or three witnesses every word may be established. And if he shall neglect to hear them, tell it unto the church; but if he neglect to hear the church, let him be unto thee as a heathen man and a publican."

Besides these sectaries, we have among us Dunkers (German *tunken*, to dip), from whom sprang the Seventh-Day Baptists of Ephratah, with their Brother and Sister houses of Celibates.

Also at Litiz we have the Moravian Church and Gottesacker (or churchyard), and a Moravian Church at Lancaster. Here, according to custom, a love-feast was held recently, when a

cup of coffee and a rusk (sweet biscuit) were
handed to each person present.*

POLITICS.

As our county was represented in Congress
by Thaddeus Stevens, you have some idea of
what our politics are. We have returned about
five or six thousand majority for the Whig, Anti-
Masonic, and Republican ticket, and the adjoining *very* "Dutch" county of Berks invariably as
great a majority for the Democratic. So striking
a difference has furnished much ground for specu-
lation. The Hon. Mr. S. says that Berks is
Democratic because so many Hessians settled
there after the Revolution. "No," says the
Hon. Mr. B., "I attribute it to the fact that the
people are not taught by unpaid ministers, as

---

* Rupp estimated (1844) that there were seven Lutheran
ministers living in the county, and that there were twenty-
seven Lutheran places for public worship. He says, "The
German Reformed have twenty places of public worship."

We have a number of "Dutch Methodists," or "Albrechts-
leute" (Albrechts people), to whom is given the name "Evangelical Association."

A young Lutheran minister has estimated that there are
over thirty religious divisions in this county, but some of them
are very small.

Rupp, who gives about twenty-two divisions (1844), says
that there is no spot upon earth, with so limited a population,
and the same confined territory, that counts more denominations than Lancaster County.

with us, but are Lutherans and German Reformed, and can be led by their preachers."
"Why is Berks Democratic?" I asked our Democratic postmaster. "I do not know," said he; "but the people here are ignorant; they do not read a paper on the other side." A former postmaster tells me that he has heard that the people of Berks were greatly in favor of liberty in the time of the elder Adams; that they put up liberty-poles, and Adams sent soldiers among them and had the liberty-poles cut down; and "ever since they have been opposèd to that political party, under its different names."*

---

* Since the above was written, a gentleman of Reading has told me that he heard James Buchanan express, in the latter part of his life, a similar opinion to one given above. Mr. Buchanan said, in effect, that while peace sects prevailed in Lancaster County, in Berks were found many Lutherans and German Reformed, who were more liberal.

The Hon. Mr. S. cited above is John Strohm. The troubles alluded to in Berks seem to have been principally on account of a direct tax, called "The House-tax," imposed during the administration of John Adams.

"The assessors were resisted, and chased from township to township. To quell the insurrection, troops were raised in *Lancaster County*, who marched to Reading and took down liberty-poles that had been erected by certain persons.

"Returning afterwards from Northampton County, they entered the office of the German 'Adler,' or 'Eagle,' and took the editor before their commanding officer, who ordered that he should receive twenty-five lashes, in the market-house, on account of certain offensive articles that had appeared in his

FESTIVALS.

The greatest festive occasion, or the one which calls the greatest number of persons to eat and drink together, is the funeral.

My friends Jacob and Susanna E. have that active benevolence and correct principle which prompt to care for the sick and dying, and kind offices toward the mourner. Nor are they alone in this. When a death occurs, our "Dutch" neighbors enter the house, and, taking possession, relieve the family as far as possible from the labors and cares of a funeral. Some "redd up" the house, making that which was neglected during the sad trials of a fatal disease, again in order for the reception of company. Others visit the kitchen, and help to bake great store of bread, pies, and rusks for the expected gathering. Two young men and two young women generally sit up together overnight to watch in a room adjoining that of the dead.

At funerals occurring on Sunday, three hundred carriages have been seen in attendance; and so great at all times is the concourse of

---

paper. As these were being inflicted, certain gentlemen interposed and prevented the carrying out of the sentence.

"Some of the insurrectionists were tried, and some condemned to death, but this sentence was not executed."

This account is taken from Rupp's *History of Berks and Lebanon Counties.*

people of all stations and all shades of belief, and so many partake of the entertainment liberally provided, that I may be excused for calling funerals the great festivals of the "Dutch." (Weddings are also highly festive occasions, but they are confined to the "Freundschaft," and to much smaller numbers.)

The services at funerals are generally conducted in the German language.

An invitation is extended to the persons present to return to eat after the funeral, or the meal is provided before leaving for the graveyard. Hospitality, in all rural districts, where the guests come from afar, seems to require this. The tables are sometimes set in a barn, or large wagon-house, and relays of guests succeed one another, until all are done. The neighbors wait upon the table. The entertainment generally consists of meat, frequently cold; bread and butter; pickles or sauces, such as apple-butter; pies and rusks; sometimes stewed chickens, mashed potatoes, cheese, etc., and coffee invariably. All depart after the dish-washing, and the family is left in quiet again.

I have said that persons of all shades of belief attend funerals; but our New Mennists are not permitted to listen to the sermons of other denominations. Memorial stones over the dead are more conspicuous than among Friends. But they are still quite plain, with simple inscrip-

3*

tions. Occasionally family graveyards are seen. One on a farm adjoining ours seems cut out of the side of a field. It stands back from the highroad, and access to it is on foot. To those who are anxious to preserve the remains of their relatives, these graveyards are objectionable, as they will probably be obliterated after the property has passed into another family.

WEDDINGS.

Our farmer had a daughter married lately, and I was invited to see the bride leave home. The groom, in accordance with the early habits of the "Dutch" folks, reached the bride's house about six A.M., having previously breakfasted and ridden four miles. As he probably fed and harnessed his horse, besides attiring himself for the grand occasion, he must have been up betimes of an October morning.

The bride wore purple mousseline-de-laine and a blue bonnet. As some of the "weddingfolks" were dilatory, the bride and groom did not get off before seven. The bridegroom was a mechanic. The whole party was composed of four couples, who rode to Lancaster in buggies, where two pairs were married by a minister. In the afternoon, the newly-married couples went down to Philadelphia for a few days; and on the evening that they were expected at home, we had a reception, or home-coming. Supper consisted of roast turkeys, beef, and stewed chickens, cakes, pies, and coffee of course. We had raisin-pie, which is a great treat in "Dutchland" on festive or solemn occasions. "Nine couples" of the bridal party sat down to supper, and then the remaining spare seats were occupied by the landlord's wife, the bride's uncle, etc. We had a fiddler in the evening. He and the dancing would not have been there, had the household "belonged to meeting;" and, as it was, some young Methodist girls did not dance.

One of my "English" acquaintances was sitting alone on a Sunday evening, when she heard a rap at the door, and a young "Dutchman," a stranger, walked in and sat down, " and there he sot, and sot, and sot." Mrs. G. waited to hear his errand, politely making conversation; and finally he asked whether her daughter was at home. "Which one?" He did not know. But that did not make much difference, as neither was at home. Mrs. G. afterwards mentioned this circumstance to a worthy "Dutch" neighbor, expressing surprise that a young man should call who had not been introduced. " How then *would* they get acquainted?" said he. She suggested that she did not think that her daughter knew the young man. "She would not tell you, perhaps, if she did." The daughter, however, when asked, seemed entirely ignorant, and did not know that she had ever seen the young man. He had probably seen her at the railroad station, and had found out her name and residence. It would seem to indicate much confidence on the part of parents, if, when acquaintances are formed in such a manner, the father and mother retire at nine o'clock, and leave their young daughter thus to "keep company," until midnight or later. It is no wonder that one of our German sects has declared against the popular manner of "courting."

I recently attended a New Mennist wedding, which took place in the frame meeting-house. We entered through an adjoining brick dwelling, one room of which served as an ante-room, where the "sisters" left their bonnets and shawls. I was late, for the services had begun about nine, on a bitter Sunday morning of December. The meeting-house was crowded, and in front on the left was a plain of book-muslin caps on the heads of the sisters. On shelves and pegs, along the other side, were placed the hats and overcoats of the brethren. The building was extremely simple,—whitewashed without, entirely unpainted within, with whitewashed walls. The preacher stood at a small, unpainted desk, and before it was a table, convenient for the old men "to sit at and lay their books on." Two stoves, a half-dozen hanging tin candlesticks, and the benches, completed the furniture. The preacher was speaking extemporaneously in English, for in this meeting-house the services are often performed in this tongue; and he spoke readily and well, though his speech was not free from such expressions as, "It would be wishful for men to do their duty;" "Man cannot separate them together;" and "This, Christ done for us."

He spoke at length upon divorce, which, he said, could not take place between Christians. The preacher spoke especially upon the duty of the wife to submit to the husband, whenever differences of sentiment arose; of the duty of the husband to love the wife, and to show his love by his readiness to assist her. He alluded to Paul's saying that it is better to be unmarried than married, and he did not scruple to use plain language touching adultery. His discourse ended, he called upon the pair proposing marriage to come forward; whereupon the man and woman rose from the body of the congregation on either side, and, coming out to the middle aisle, stood together before the minister. They had both passed their early youth, but had very good faces. The bride wore a mode-colored alpaca, and a black apron; also a clear-starched cap without a border, after the fashion of the sect. The groom wore a dark-green coat, cut "shad-bellied," after the manner of the brethren.

This was probably the manner of their acquaintance: If, in spite of Paul's encouragement to a single life, a brother sees a sister whom he wishes to marry, he mentions the fact to a minister, who tells it to the sister. If she agrees in sentiment, the acquaintance continues for a year, during which private interviews can be had, if desired; but this sect entirely discourages courting as usually practiced among the "Dutch."

The year having in this case elapsed, and the pair having now met before the preacher, he propounded to them three questions:

1. I ask of this brother, as the bridegroom, do you believe that this sister in the faith is allotted to you by God as your helpmeet and spouse? And I ask of you, as the bride, do you believe that this your brother is allotted to you by God as your husband and head?

2. Are you free in your affections from all others, and have you them centred alone upon this your brother or sister?

3. Do you receive this person as your lawfully wedded husband [wife], do you promise to be faithful to him [her], to reverence him [to love her], and that nothing but death shall separate you; that, by the help of God, you will, to the best of your ability, fulfill all the duties which God has enjoined on believing husbands and wives?

In answering this last question, I observed the bride to lift her eyes to the preacher's face, as if in fearless trust. Then the preacher, directing them to join hands, pronounced them man and wife, and invoked a blessing upon them. This was followed by a short prayer, after which the wedded pair separated, each again taking a place among the congregation. The occasion was solemn. On resuming his place in the desk, the preacher's eyes were seen to be suffused, and pocket-handkerchiefs were visible on either side (the sisters' white, those of the brethren of colored silk). The audience then knelt, while the preacher prayed, and I heard responses like those of the Methodists, but more subdued. The preacher made a few remarks, to the effect that, although it would be grievous to break the bond now uniting these two, it would be infinitely more grievous to break the tie which unites us to Christ; and then a quaint hymn was sung to a familiar tune. The "Church" does not allow wedding-parties, but a few friends may gather at the house after meeting.

The marriage ceremony among the Amish is performed, it is said, in meeting.

One of my neighbors has told me that the Amish "have great fun at weddings;" that they have a table set all night, and that when the weather is pleasant, they play in the barn. "Our Peter went once," she continued, "with a lot of the public-school scholars. They let them go in and look on. They twisted a towel for the bloom-sock, and they did hit each other."

(Bloom-sock, *Plump-sack*, a twisted kerchief, —a clumsy fellow.)

"The bloom-sock" (*oo* short), as one of my acquaintances described it, "is a handkerchief twisted long, from the two opposite corners. When it is twisted, you double it, and tie the ends with a knot. One in front hunts the handkerchief, and those on the bench are passing it behind them.´ If they get a chance, they'll hit him with it, and if he sees it, he tears it away. Then he goes into the row, and the other goes out to hunt it."

"The English folks have a game like that," said I. "We call it 'Hunt the Slipper.'"

It has also been said that at Amish wedding-parties they do what they call *Glücktrinke*, of wine, etc.

Some wedding-parties are called Infares. Thus, a neighbor spoke of "Siegfried's wedding, where they had such an Infare."

It must not be supposed from these descriptions that we have no "fashionable" persons among us, of the old German stock. When they have become fashionable, however, they do not desire to be called "Dutch."

QUILTINGS.

Some ten years ago there came to our neighborhood a pleasant, industrious "Aunt Sally," a "yellow woman;" and the other day she had a quilting, for she had long wished to re-cover two quilts. The first who arrived at Aunt Sally's was our neighbor from over the "creek," or mill-stream, Polly M., in her black silk Mennist bonnet, formed like a sun-bonnet; and at ten came my dear friend Susanna E., who is tall and fat, and very pleasant;

> "Whose heart has a look southward, and is open
> To the great noon of nature."

Aunt Sally had her quilt up in her landlord's east room, for her own house was too small. However, at about eleven she called us over to dinner; for people who have breakfasted at five or six have an appetite at eleven.

We found on the table beefsteaks, boiled pork, sweet potatoes, kohl-slaw,* pickled tomatoes, cucumbers, and *red* beets (thus the "Dutch" accent lies), apple-butter and preserved peaches, pumpkin and apple pie, sponge-cake and coffee.

---

* Kohl-slaw (*i.e.* Kohl-salat or Cabbage-salad?) is shredded cabbage, dressed with vinegar, etc. A rich dressing is sometimes made of milk or cream, egg, vinegar, etc.. It may be eaten either as warm slaw or cold slaw.

4

After dinner came our next neighbors, " the maids," Susy and Katy Groff, who live in single blessedness and great neatness. They wore pretty, clear-starched Mennist caps, very plain. Katy is a sweet-looking woman ; and, although she is more than sixty years old, her forehead is almost unwrinkled, and her fine fair hair is still brown. It was late when the farmer's wife came, —three o'clock ; for she had been to Lancaster. She wore hoops, and was of the " world's people." These women all spoke "Dutch;" for "the maids," whose ancestor came here probably one hundred and fifty years ago, do not speak English with fluency yet.

The first subject of conversation was the fall house-cleaning; and I heard mention of "die carpett hinaus an der fence," and " die fenshter und die porch ;" and the exclamation, " My goodness, es war schlimm." I quilted faster than Katy Groff, who showed me her hands, and said, " You have not been corn-husking, as I have."

So we quilted and rolled, talked and laughed, got one quilt done, and put in another. The work was not fine; we laid it out by chalking around a small plate. Aunt Sally's desire was rather to get her quilting finished upon this great occasion, than for us to put in a quantity of needlework.

About five o'clock we were called to supper. I need not tell you all the particulars of this plentiful meal. But the stewed chicken was tender, and we had coffee again.

Polly M.'s husband now came over the creek in the boat, to take her home, and he warned her against the evening dampness. The rest of us quilted awhile by candle and lamp, and got the second quilt done at about seven.

At this quilting there was little gossip, and less scandal. I displayed my new alpaca, and my dyed merino, and the Philadelphia bonnet which exposes the back of my head to the wintry blast. Polly, for her part, preferred a black silk sun-bonnet; and so we parted, with mutual invitations to visit.

FARMING.

In this fertile limestone district, farming is very laborious, being entirely by tillage. Our regular routine is once in five years to plow the sod ground for corn. In the next ensuing year the same ground is sowed with oats; and when the oats come off in August, the industrious "Dutchmen" immediately manure the stubble-land for wheat. I have seen them laying the dark-brown heaps upon the yellow stubble when, in August, I have ridden some twelve or four-teen miles down to the hill-country for black-berries.

After the ground is carefully prepared, wheat

and timothy (grass) seed are put in with a drill, and in the ensuing spring clover is sowed upon the same ground. By July, when the wheat is taken off the ground, the clover and timothy are growing, and will be ready to mow in the next, or fourth summer. In the fifth, the same grass constitutes a grazing-ground, and then the sod is ready to be broken up again for Indian corn. Potatoes are seldom planted here in great quantities; a part of one of the oat-fields or corn-fields can be put into potatoes, and the ground will be ready by fall to be put into wheat, if it is desired. A successful farmer put more than half of his forty acres into wheat; this being considered the best crop. The average crop of wheat is about twenty bushels, of Indian corn about forty.

I have heard of one hundred bushels of corn in the Pequea valley, but this is very rare. When the wheat and oats are in the barn or stack, enormous eight-horse threshers,* whose owners go about the neighborhood from farm to farm, thresh the crop in two or three days; and thus what was once a great job for winter may all be finished by the 1st of October.

Jacob E. is a model farmer. His buildings and fences are in good order, and his cattle well kept. He is a little past the prime of life; his beautiful head of black hair being touched with silver.

---

* Steam-engines are now in use for threshing (1872).

His wife is dimpled and smiling, and her two hundred and twenty pounds do not prevent her being active, energetic, forehanded, and "through-going." During the winter months the two sons go to the public school,—the older one with reluctance; there they learn to read and write and "cipher," and possibly study geography; they speak English at school, and "Dutch" at home. Much education the "Dutch" farmer fears, as productive of laziness; and laziness is a mortal sin here. The E.'s rarely buy a book.* The winter is employed partly in preparing material to fertilize the wheat-land during the coming summer. Great droves of cattle and sheep come down our road from the West, and our farmers buy from these, and fatten stock during the winter months for the Philadelphia market.

A proper care of his stock will occupy some portion of the farmer's time.† Then he has generally a great "Freundschaft," or family connection, both his and his wife's; and the paying

---

* I suggested to one of my farming neighbors that he might advantageously have given a certain son a chance at books.

" Don't want no books !" was the answer. " There's enough goes to books! Get so lazy after awhile, they won't farm."

.† A young farmer's son told me also of cutting wood and quarrying stone in the winter, and added, " If a person wouldn't work in the winter, they'd be behindhand in the spring."

4*

visits within a range of twenty or thirty miles, and receiving visits in return, help to pass away the time. Then Jacob and Susanna are actively benevolent; they are liable to be called upon, summer and winter, to wait on the sick and to help bury the dead. Susanna was formerly renowned as a baker at funerals, where her services were freely given.

This rich level land of ours is highly prized by the "Dutch" for farming purposes, and the great demand has enhanced the price. The farms, too, are small, seventy acres being a fair size. When Seth R., the rich preacher, bought his last farm from an "Englishman," William G. said to him, " Well, Seth, it seems as if you Dutch folks had determined to root us English out; but thee had to pay pretty dear for thy root this time."

There are some superstitious ideas that still hold sway here, regarding the growth of plants. A young girl coming to us for cabbage-plants said that it was a good time to set them out, for "'it was in the Wirgin." It is very doubtful whether she knew *what* was in Virgo, but I suppose that it was the moon. So our farmer's wife tells me that the Virgin will do very well for cabbages, but not for any flowering plant like beans, for, though they will bloom well, they will not mature the fruit. Grain should be sowed in the increase of the moon; meat butchered in the decrease will shrink in the pot.

FARMERS' WIVES.

One of my Dutch neighbors, who, from a shoemaker, became the owner of two farms, said to me, "The woman is more than half;" and his own very laborious wife (with her portion) had indeed been so.

The woman (in popular parlance, "the old woman") milks, raises the poultry, has charge of the garden,—sometimes digging the ground herself, and planting and hoeing, with the assistance of her daughters and the "maid," when she has one. (German, *magd.*) To be sure, she does not go extensively into vegetable-raising, nor has she a large quantity of strawberries and other small fruits ; neither does she plant a great many peas and beans, that are laborious to "stick." She has a quantity of cabbages and of "red beets," of onions and of early potatoes, in her garden, a plenty of cucumbers for winter pickles, and store of string-beans and tomatoes, with some sweet potatoes.

Peter R. told me that in one year, off of their small farm, they sold "two hundred dollars' worth of *wedgable* things, not counting the butter." As in that year the clothing for each member of the family probably cost from ten to fifteen dollars, the two hundred dollars' worth of vegetable things was of great importance.

Our "Dutch" never make *store*-cheese. At a county fair, only one cheese was exhibited, and that was from Chester County. The farmer's wife boards all the farm-hands, and the mechanics,—the carpenter, mason, etc., who put up the new buildings, and the fence-makers. At times she allows the daughters to go out and husk corn. It was a pretty sight which I saw one fall day,—an Amish man with four sons and daughters, husking in the field.* "We do it all ourselves," said he.

In the winter mornings perhaps the farmer's wife goes out to milk in the stable with a lantern, while her daughters get breakfast; has her house "redd up" about eight o'clock, and is prepared for several hours' sewing before dinner, laying by great piles of shirts for summer. We no longer make linen; but I have heard of one Dutch girl who had a good supply of domestic linen made into shirts and trousers for the future spouse whose "fair proportions" she had not yet seen.

There are, of course, many garments to make in a large family, but there is not much work put

---

* Said a neighbor, "A man told me once that he was at an Amish husking,—a husking-match in the kitchen. He said he never saw as much sport in all his life. There they had the *bloom-sock*. There was one old man, quite gray-headed, and gray-bearded : he laughed till he shook." Said another, "There's not many huskings going on now. The most play now goes on at the Infares."

upon them. We do not yet patronize the sewing-machine* very extensively, but a seamstress or tailoress is sometimes called in. At the spring cleaning, the labors of the women folk are increased by whitewashing the picket-fences.

In March we make soap, before the labors of the garden are great. The forests are being obliterated from this fertile tract, and many use what some call " consecrated" lye; formerly, the ash-hopper was filled, and a good lot of. egg-bearing lye run off to begin the soap with, while the weaker filled the soft-soap kettle, after the soap had " come." The chemical operation of soap-making often proved difficult, and, of course, much was said about luck. " We had bad luck, making soap." A sassafras stick was preferred for stirring, and the soap was stirred always in one direction. In regard to this, and that other chemical operation, making and keeping vinegar, there are certain ideas about the temporary in-capacity of some persons,—ideas only to be al-luded to here. If the farmer's wife never " has luck" in making soap, she employs some skillful woman to come in and help her. It is not a long operation, for the " Dutch" rush this work speedily. If the lye is well run off, two tubs of hard soap and a barrel of soft can be made in a

---

* Sewing-machines have become common since this article was written.

day. A smart housekeeper can make a barrel
of soap in the morning, and go visiting in the
afternoon.

Great are the household labors in harvest; but
the cooking and baking in the hot weather are
cheerfully done for the men folks, who are toil-
ing in hot suns and stifling barns. Four meals
are common at this season, for " a piece" is sent
out at nine o'clock. I heard of one Dutch girl's
making some fifty pies a week in harvest; for if
you have four meals a day, and pie at each, many
are required. We have great faith in pie.

I have been told of an inexperienced Quaker
housewife in the neighboring county of York,
who was left in charge of the farm, and, during
harvest, these important labors were performed
by John Stein, John Stump, and John Stinger.
She also had guests, welcome perhaps as " rain
in harvest." To conciliate the Johns was very
important, and she waited on them first. "What
will thee have, John Stein?" "What shall I
give thee, John Stump?" "And thee, John
Stinger?" On one memorable occasion there
was mutiny in the field, for John Stein declared
that he never worked where there were not
" kickelin" cakes in harvest, nor would he now.
Küchlein proved to be cakes fried in fat; and
the housewife was ready to appease " Achilles'
wrath," as soon as she made this discovery.

We used to make quantities of apple-butter in

the fall, but of late years apples have been more scarce. We made in one season six barrels of cider into apple-butter, three at a time. Two large copper kettles were hung under the beech-trees, down between the spring-house and smoke-house, and the cider was boiled down the evening before, great stumps of trees being in demand. One hand watched the cider, and the rest of the family gathered in the kitchen and labored diligently in preparing the cut apples, so that in the morning the "schnitz" might be ready to go in. (*Schneiden*, to cut, *geschnitten*.)

Two bushels and a half of cut apples will be enough for a barrel of cider. In a few hours the apples will all be in, and then you will stir, and stir, and stir, for you do not want to have the apple-butter burn at the bottom, and be obliged to dip it out into tubs and scour the kettle. Some time in the afternoon, you will take out a little on a dish, and when you find that the cider no longer "weeps out" round the edges, but all forms a simple heap, you will dip it up into earthen vessels, and when cold take it " on" to the garret to keep company with the hard soap and the bags of dried apples and cherries, perhaps with the hams and shoulders. Soap and apple-butter are usually made in an open fireplace, where hangs the kettle. At one time (about the year 1828) I have heard that there was apple-butter in the Lancaster Museum which dated from Revolutionary times; for we do not expect it to ferment in the summer. It dries away; but water is stirred in to prepare it for the table. Sometimes peach-butter is made, with cider, molasses, or sugar, and, in the present scarcity of apples, cut pump-kin is often put into the apple-butter.*

Soon after apple-butter-making comes butcher-ing, for we like an early pig in the fall, when the store of smoked meat has run out. Pork is the staple, and we smoke the flitches, not preserv-

---

* Evening "Snitzen" parties and apple-butter-boilings have been festive occasions. A young mechanic was telling me of the games that he had joined in after the apples were cut, etc., and added, "How I have enjoyed myself!"

Mr. E. H. Rauch, who has lived also in Berks County, thus describes an apple-butter party:

"Then Bevvy (Barbara) came and sat down in the very chair that Sally had left opposite, saying, 'I'll sit here. I am not afraid of Pete, and I guess that he is not afraid of me.' She was thought to be a very smart girl, and earned good wages, and she was quite pretty too, and nice-looking. As we were paring apples, once in awhile she handed me over a piece, which did not offend me, and she looked and talked so pleasant, that I began to think a good deal of her. When the apple-paring was done, then we must stir the apple-butter. Commonly, a boy and girl both take hold of the long handle of the stirrer, and stir together with a sort of see-saw motion, so that I have been ready to go to sleep with the stirrer in my hand.

"In the course of the evening, Bevvy and I stirred together three different times, and got very well acquainted. Then I took her home, and there was no cross old thing to come and say, 'It is time to go,' as Sally Bensamacher's father did one time."—*Letters of Pete Schwefflebrenner.*

ing them in brine like the Yankees. We ourselves use much beef, and do not like smoked
flitch, but I speak for the majority. Sausage is
a great dish with us, as in Germany. My sister
and I went once on a few days' trip through the
county in the summer, and were treated alter-
nately to ham and mackerel, until, at the last
house, we had both.

Butchering is one of the many occasions for
the display of friendly feeling, when brother or
father steps in to help hang the hogs, or a sister
to assist in rendering lard, or in preparing the
plentiful meal. An active farmer will have two
or three porkers killed, scalded, and hung up by
sunrise, and by night the whole operation of
sausage and "scrapple" making, and lard rendering, will be finished, and the house set in
order. The friends who have assisted receive a
portion of the sausage, etc., which portion is
called the "Metzel-sup."* The metzel-sup is also
sent to poor widows, and others.

We make scrapple from the skin, a part of the
livers, and heads, with the addition of corn-meal ;
but, instead, our "Dutch" neighbors make *liver-
wurst* ("woorsht"), or meat pudding, omitting the
meal, and this compound, stuffed into the larger
entrails, is very popular in Lancaster market.
Some make *pawn-haus* from the liquor in which

---

* Pronounce sup, *soup*, with the *oo* short.

5

the pudding-meat was boiled, adding thereto corn-meal. These three dishes are fried before eating. I have never seen hog's-head cheese in "Dutch" houses. If the boiling-pieces of beef are kept over summer, they are smoked, instead of being preserved in brine. We eat much smear-case (*Schmier-käse*), or cottage cheese, in these regions. Children, and some grown people too, fancy it upon bread with molasses; which may be considered as an offset to the Yankee pork and molasses.

We have also Dutch cheese, which may be made by crumbling the dry smear-case, working in butter, salt, and chopped sage, forming it into pats, and setting them away to ripen. The *sieger-käse* is made from sweet milk boiled, with sour milk added and beaten eggs, and then set to drain off the whey. (*Ziegen-käse* is German for goat's milk cheese.)

"Schnitz and knep" is said to be made of dried apples, fat pork, and dough-dumplings cooked together.

In the fall our "Dutch" make *sauer kraut*. I happened into the house of my friend Susanna when her husband and son were going to take an hour at noon to help her with the kraut. Two white tubs stood upon the back porch, one with the fair round heads, and the other to receive the cabbage when cut by a knife set in a board (a very convenient thing for cutting kohl-slaw and cucum-

bers). When cut, the cabbage is packed into a
" stand" with a sauer-kraut staff, resembling the
pounder with which New-Englanders beat clothes
in a barrel. Salt is added during the packing.
When the cabbage ferments, it becomes acid.
The kraut-stand remains in the cellar; the contents not being unpalatable when boiled with
potatoes and the chines or ribs of pork. But the
smell of the boiling kraut is very strong, and
that stomach is probably strong which readily
digests the meal.*

Our "Dutch" make soup in variety, and pronounce the word short, between *soup* and *sup*.
Thus there is Dutch sup, potato sup, and
" noodle" (*Nudel*) sup,—which last is a treat.
Nudels may be called domestic macaroni; and
I have seen a dish called *schmelkty-nudels*, in which
bits of fried bread were laid upon the piled-
up nudels,—to me unpalatable from the large
quantity of eggs in the nudels.

We almost always find good bread at our farm-

---

* One of the heavy labors of the fall is the fruit-drying.
Afterward your hostess invites you to partake, thus : " Mary,
will you have pie? This is snits, and this is elder" (or dried
apples, and dried elderberries).

Dried peaches are peach snits.

A laboring woman once, speaking to me of a neighbor, said,
" She hain't got many dried apples. If her girl would snitz
in the evening, as I did !—but she'd rather keep company and
run around than to snitz."

houses. In traveling through Pennsylvania to Ohio, and returning through New York, I concluded that Pennsylvania furnished good bread-makers, New York good butter-makers, and that the two best bread-makers that I saw in Ohio were from Lancaster County. We make the pot of "sots" (New England "emptins") overnight, with boiled mashed potatoes, scalded flour, and sometimes hops. Friday is baking-day; but in the middle of summer, when mold abounds, we bake twice a week. The "Dutch" housewife is very fond of baking in the brick oven, but the scarcity of wood must gradually accustom us to the great cooking-stove.

We keep one fire in winter. This is in the kitchen, which with nice housekeepers is the abode of neatness, with its rag carpet and brightly polished stove. An adjoining room or building is the wash-house, where butchering, soap-making, etc. are done by the help of a great kettle hung in the fireplace, not set in brick-work.

Adjoining the kitchen, on another side, is a state apartment, also rag-carpeted, and called "the room." The stove-pipe from the kitchen sometimes passes through the ceiling, and tempers the sleeping-room of the parents. These arrangements are not very favorable to bathing in cold weather; indeed, to wash the whole person is not very common, in summer or winter.

In the latter season, it is almost never done in town or country, by the "Dutch."*

Will you go up-stairs in a neat Dutch farmhouse? Here are rag carpets again. Gay quilts are on the best beds, where green and red calico, perhaps in the form of a basket, are displayed on a white ground; or the beds bear brilliant coverlets of red, white, and blue, as if to " make the rash gazer wipe his eye." The common pillowcases are sometimes of blue check, or of calico. In winter, people often sleep under feather-covers, not so heavy as a feather-bed. In the spring there is a great washing of bedclothes, and then the blankets are washed, which, during winter, supplied the place of sheets.

HOLIDAYS.

I was sitting alone, one Christmas time, when the door opened and there entered some half-dozen youths or men, who frightened me so that I slipped out at the door. They, being thus alone, and not intending further harm, at once left. These, I suppose, were Christmas mummers, though I heard them called " Bell-schnickel."

At another time, as I was sitting with my little boy, Aunt Sally came in smiling and mysterious, and took her place by the stove. Immediately

---

* Is it done very often by our English farming population?

5*

after, there entered a man in disguise, who very much alarmed my little Dan.

The stranger threw down nuts and cakes, and, when some one offered to pick them up, struck at him with a rod. This was the real Bell-schnickel, personated by the farmer. I presume that he ought to throw down his store of nice things for the good children, and strike the bad ones with his whip. Pelznickel is the bearded Nicholas, who punishes bad ones; whereas Kriss-kringle is the Christkindlein, who rewards good children.

On Christmas morning we cry, " Christmas-gift !" and not, as elsewhere, " A merry Christ-mas !" Christmas is a day when people do not work, but go to meeting, when roast turkey and mince-pie are in order, and when the "Dutch" housewife has store of cakes on hand to give to the little folks.

We still hear of barring-out at Christmas. The pupils fasten themselves in the school-house, and keep the teacher out to obtain presents from him.

The First of April (which our neighbors gen-erally call Aprile) is a great occasion. This is the opening of the farming year. The tenant farmers and other " renters" move to their new homes, and interest-money and other debts are due; and so much money changes hands in Lan-caster, on the 1st, that pickpockets are attracted thither, and the unsuspicious "Dutch" farmer sometimes finds himself a loser.

The movings, on or about the 1st, are made festive occasions; neighbors, young and old, are gathered; some bring wagons to transport farm utensils and furniture, others assist in driving cattle, put furniture in its place, and set up bedsteads; while the women are ready to help prepare the bountiful meal. At this feast I have heard a worthy tenant farmer say, "Now help yourselves, as you did out there" (with the goods).

Whitsuntide Monday is a great holiday with the young "Dutch" folks. It occurs when there is a lull in farm-work, between corn-planting and hay-making. Now the new summer bonnets are all in demand, and the taverns are found full of youths and girls, who sometimes walk the street hand-in-hand, eat cakes and drink beer, or visit the "flying horses." A number of seats are arranged around a central pole, and, a pair taking each seat, the whole revolves by the work of a horse, and you can have a *circular* ride for six cents.

On the Fourth of July we are generally at work in the harvest-field. Several of the festivals of the Church are held here as days of rest, if not of recreation. Such are Good Friday, Ascension-day, etc. On Easter, eggs colored and otherwise ornamented were formerly much in vogue; but the custom of preparing them is dying out.*

Thanksgiving is beginning to be observed here, but the New-Englander would miss the family gatherings, the roast turkeys, the pumpkin-pies. Possibly we go to church in the morning, and sit quiet for the rest of the day; and as for pumpkin-pies, we do not greatly fancy them. Raisin-pie, or mince-pie, we can enjoy.

The last night of October is " Hallow-eve." I was in Lancaster last Hallow-eve, and the boys were ringing door-bells, carrying away door-steps, throwing corn at the windows, or running off with an unguarded wagon. I heard of one

---

* A neighbor has told me that the people here used to make fat-cakes—they called them "plow-lines"—on Shrove-Tuesday, or else " they conceited the flax wouldn't grow. The people used to conceit a many things," she added. Nor is the custom of baking pancakes on Shrove-Tuesday yet given up. A correspondent of the *Reading Eagle*, of February 16th, 1872, says, " Tuesday was a great day among our county women (Berks County) for manufacturing doughnuts. In every house we entered we found the good wife engaged in some part of the baking performance; . . . and later in the day we saw heaps of the delicious nuts piled up for table use. Such are the old usages of 'Fastnacht,' and I move they be continued."

Similar reports came in also from York and Lancaster Counties; while a Lancaster correspondent, speaking of the next day, says, "Seven years ago, I witnessed a sale of a large stock of cattle, on Ash-Wednesday: every cow and steer offered for sale was completely covered with wood ashes."

or two youngsters who had requested an afternoon holiday to go to church, but who had spent
their time in going out of town to steal corn for
this occasion. In the country, farm-gates are
taken from their hinges and removed; and it was
formerly a favorite boyish amusement to take a
wagon to pieces, and, after carrying the parts up
to the barn-roof, to put it together again, thus
obliging the owner to take it apart and bring it
down. Such "tricks" as described by Burns in
the poem of "Hallow-e'en" may be heard of occasionally, perpetrated perhaps by the Scotch-
Irish element in our population.

PUBLIC SCHOOLS.

About twenty years ago, I was circulating an
anti-slavery petition among women. I carried it
to the house of a neighboring farmer, a miller to
boot, and well to do. His wife signed the petition (*all* women did not in those days), but she
signed with her mark. I have understood that
it is about twenty years since the school law was
made universal here, and that our township of
Upper Leacock wanted to resist by litigation
the establishment of public schools, but finally
decided otherwise.* It is the school-tax that is

---

* In a recent paper I find this statement: "West Cocalico
did not until recently accept the provisions of the General
School Law of the State."

onerous. Within the last twenty years a great impetus has been given to education by the establishment of the County Superintendency of Normal Schools and of Teachers' Institutes. I think it is within this time that the Board of Directors met, in an adjoining township, and, being called upon to vote by ballot, there were afterward found in the box several different ways of spelling the word " no."

At the last Institute, a worthy young man at the blackboard was telling the teachers how to make their pupils pronounce the word "did," which they inclined to call *dit;* and a young woman told me that she found it necessary, when teaching in Berks County, to practice speaking "Dutch," in order to make the pupils understand their lessons. It must be rather hard to hear and talk "Dutch" almost constantly, and then go to a school where the text-books are English.

There is still an effort made to have German taught in our public schools. The reading of German is considered a great accomplishment, and is one required for a candidate for the ministry among some of our plainer sects. But the teacher is generally overburdened in the winter with the *necessary* branches in a crowded, ungraded school. Our township generally has school for seven months in the year; some townships have only five; and in Berks County I have heard of one having only four months.

About thirty-five dollars a month is paid to teachers, male and female.

My little boy of seven began to go to public school this fall. For awhile I would hear him repeating such expressions as, " Che, double o, t, coot" (meaning good). "P-i-g, pick." "Kreat A, little A, pouncing P." "I don't like chincher-pread." Even among our "Dutch" people of more culture, *etch* is heard for *aitch* (H), and it is a relic of early training.

The standard of our County Superintendent is high (1868), and his examinations are severe. His salary is about seventeen hundred dollars. Where there is so much wealth as here, it seems almost impossible that learning should not follow, as soon as the minds of the people are turned toward it; but the great fear of making their children "lazy" operates against sending them to school. Industrious habits will certainly tend more to the pecuniary success of a farmer than the "art of writing and speaking the English language *correctly.*"*

---

* The story of the difficulties that have beset those who have striven to introduce the public school system in some parts of Pennsylvania is a remarkable one. In the county of Berks (as well as in Lancaster), it is claimed that the Reformed and Lutheran settlers had schools, in early times, in connection with their churches; but as regards the public schools, Berks is now considerably behind Lancaster.

The fear of making the children lazy, as it seems to me now,

MANNERS AND CUSTOMS.

My dear old "English" friend, Samuel G., had often been asked to stay and eat with David B., and on one occasion he concluded to accept the invitation. They went to the table, and had a silent pause; then John cut up the meat, and the workmen and members of the family each put in a fork and helped himself. The guest was discomfited, and, finding that he was likely to lose his dinner otherwise, he followed their example. The invitation to eat had covered the whole. When guests are present, many say, "Now, help yourselves," but they do not use vain repetitions, as the city people do.

Coffee is still drunk three times a day in some

---

is not the only objection to the public schools in the minds of some of our "Pennsylvania Dutch."

An Amish man (who labored under the difficulty of not speaking English fluently) once answered some of my inquiries upon the subject of education.

He said that they were not opposed to school-learning, but to high learning. "To send children to school from ten to twenty-one, we would think was opposed to Holy Scripture. There are things taught in school that don't agree with Holy Scripture."

I asked whether he thought it was wrong to teach that the earth goes round the sun.

"I don't know anything about it; but I am not in favor of teaching geography and grammar in the schools: it's worldly wisdom."

families, but frequently without sugar. The sugar-bowl stands on the table, with spoons therein for those who want sugar ; but at our late " home-coming" party I believe that I was the only one at the table who took sugar. The dishes of smear-case, molasses, apple-butter, etc. are not always supplied with spoons. *We* dip in our knives, and with the same useful implements convey the food to our mouths. Does the opposite extreme prevail among the farmers of Massachusetts? Do they always eat with their forks, and use napkins?

On many busy farm-occasions, the woman of the house will find it more convenient to let the men eat first,—to get the burden of the harvest-dinner off her mind and her hands, and then sit down with her daughters, her "maid" and little children, to their own repast. But the allowing to the men the constant privilege of eating first has passed away, if, indeed, it ever prevailed. At funeral feasts the old men and women sit down first, with the mourning family. Then succeed the second, third, and fourth tables.

We Lancaster "Dutch" are always striving to seize Time's forelock. We rise, even in the win-ter, about four, feed the stock while the women get breakfast, eat breakfast in the short days by coal-oil lamps, and by daylight are ready for the operations of the day. The English folks and the backsliding "Dutch" are sometimes startled when

6

they hear their neighbors blow the horn or ring the bell for dinner. On a recent pleasant October day, the farmer's wife was churning out-of-doors, and cried, " Why, there's the dinner-bells a'ready. Mercy days!" I went in to the clock, and found it at twenty minutes of eleven. The "Dutch" farmers almost invariably keep their time half an hour or more ahead, like that village of Cornwall where it was twelve o'clock when it was but half-past eleven to the rest of the world. Our "Dutch" are never seen running to catch a railroad train.

We are not a total-abstinence people. Before these times of high prices, liquor was often furnished to hands in the harvest-field.

A few years ago a meeting was held in a neighboring school-house, to discuss a prohibitory liquor law. After various speeches, the question was put to the vote, thus: " All those who want leave to drink whisky will please to rise." "Now all those who don't want to drink whisky will rise." The affirmative had a decided majority.

Work is a cardinal virtue with the "Dutchman." " He is lazy," is a very opprobrious remark. At the quilting, when I was trying to take out one of the screws, Katy Groff, who is sixty-five, exclaimed, " How lazy I am, not to be helping you!" (" Wie ich bin faul.")

Marriages sometimes take place between the

two nationalities; but I do not think the "Dutch" farmers desire English wives for their sons, unless the wives are decidedly rich. On the other hand, I heard of an English farmer's counseling his son to seek a "Dutch" wife. When the son had wooed and won his substantial bride, "Now he will see what good cooking is," said a "Dutch" girl to me. I was surprised at the remark, for his mother was an excellent housekeeper.

The circus is the favorite amusement of our people. Lancaster papers often complain of the slender attendance which is bestowed upon lectures, and the like. Even theatrical performances are found "slow," compared with the feats of the ring.

Our "Dutch" use a freedom of language that is not known to the English, and which to them savors of coarseness. "But they mean no harm by it," says one of my English friends. It is difficult to practice reserve where the whole family sit in one heated room. This rich limestone land in which the "Dutch" delight is nearly level to an eye trained among the hills. Do hills make a people more poetical or imaginative?

Perhaps so; but there is vulgarity too among the hills.

AN AMISH MEETING.[*]

It was on a Sunday morning in March, when the air was bleak and the roads were execrable, that I obtained a driver to escort me to the farm-house where an Amish meeting was to be held.

It was a little after nine o'clock when I entered, and, although the hour was so early, I found the congregation nearly all gathered, and the preaching begun.

There were forty men present, as many women, and one infant. Had the weather been less inclement, we should probably have had more little ones, for such plain people do not think it necessary to leave the babies at home.

The rooms in which we sat seemed to have been constructed for these great occasions. They were the kitchen and "the room,"—as our people call the sitting-room, or best room,—and were so arranged as to be made into one by means of two doors.

Our neighbors wore the usual costume of the sect, which is a branch of the Mennonite So-

---

[*] Amish is pronounced *Ommish*, the *a* being very broad, like *aw*.

ciety, or nearly allied to it, the men having laid off their round-crowned and remarkably wide-brimmed hats. Their hair is usually cut square across the forehead, and hangs long behind; their coats are plainer than those of the plainest Quaker, and are fastened, except the overcoat, with hooks and eyes in place of buttons; whence they are sometimes called Hooker or Hook-and-Eye Mennists. The pantaloons are worn without suspenders. Formerly, the Amish were often called Beardy Men, but since beards have become fashionable theirs are not so conspicuous.

The women, whom I have sometimes seen with a bright-purple apron, an orange necker-chief, or some other striking bit of color, were now more soberly arrayed in plain white caps without ruffle or border, and white neckerchiefs, though occasionally a cap or kerchief was black. They wear closely-fitting waists, with a little basquine behind, which is probably a relic from the times of the short-gown and petticoat. Their gowns were of sober woolen stuff, frequently of flannel; and all wore aprons.

But the most surprising figures among the Amish are the little children, dressed in garments like those of old persons. It has been my lot to see at the house of her parents a tender little dark-eyed Amish maiden of three years, old enough to begin to speak "Dutch," and as yet ignorant of English. Seated upon

6*

her father's lap, sick and suffering, with that sweet little face encircled by the plain muslin cap, the little figure dressed in that plain gown, she was one not to be soon forgotten. But the little girl that was at meeting to-day was either no Amish child or a great backslider, for she was hardly to be distinguished in dress from the world's people.

The floors were bare, but on one of the open doors hung a long white towel, worked at one end with colored figures, such as our mothers or grandmothers put upon samplers. These perhaps were meant for flowers. The congregation sat principally on benches. On the men's side a small shelf of books ran around one corner of the room.

The preacher, who was speaking when I entered, continued for about fifteen minutes. His remarks and the rest of the services were in "Dutch." I have been criticised for applying the epithet to my neighbors, or to their language, but "Dutch" is the title which they generally apply to themselves, speaking of "us Dutch folks and you English folks," and sometimes with a pretty plain hint that some of the "Dutch" ways are discreeter and better, if not more virtuous, than the English. But, though I call them "Dutch," I am fully aware that they are not Hollanders. Most of them are Swiss of

ancient and honorable descent, exiles from religious persecution.

I am sorry that I do not understand the language well enough to give a sketch of some of
the discourses on this occasion. At times I understood an expression of the first speaker, such
as, "Let us well reflect and observe," or "Let
us well consider," expressions that were often
repeated. As he was doubtless a farmer, and
was speaking extemporaneously, it is not remarkable that they were so.

When the preacher had taken his seat, the
congregation knelt for five minutes in silence.
A brother then read aloud from the German
Scripture concerning Nicodemus, who came to
Jesus by night, etc. After this another brother
rose, and spoke in a tone like that which is so
common among Friends, namely, a kind of singing or chanting tone, which he accompanied by
a little gesture.

While he was speaking, one or two women
went out, and, as I wished to take notes of the
proceedings, I followed them into the wash-
house or outside kitchen, which was quite comfortable. As I passed along, I saw in the yard
the wagons which had brought the people to
meeting. Most of them were covered with
plain yellow oil-cloth. I have been told that
there are sometimes a hundred wagons gath-

ered at one farm-house, and that in summer the meetings are often held in the barn.

I sat down by the stove in the wash-house, and a very kindly old woman, the host's mother, came and renewed the fire. As she did not talk English, I spoke to her a little in German, and she seemed to understand me. When I wrote, she wondered and laughed at my rapid movements, for writing is slower work with these people than some other kinds of labor. I suppose, indeed, that there are still some of the older women who scarcely know how to write.

I asked her whether after meeting I might look at the German books on the corner shelf,— ancient books with dark leather covers and metallic clasps. She said in reply, " Bleibsht esse ?" ("Shall you stay and eat ?") Yes, I would. "Ya wohl," said she, "kannsht." ("Very well, you can.")

A neat young Amish woman, the "maid" or housekeeper, came and put upon the stove a great tin wash-boiler, shining bright, into which she put water for making coffee and for washing dishes.

I soon returned to the meeting, and found the same preacher still speaking. I suppose that he had continued during my absence, and, if so, his discourse was an hour and ten minutes in length. This was quite too long to be entertaining to one who only caught the sense of an occasional passage, or a few texts of Scripture. It was while these monotonous tones continued that I heard a rocking upon the floor overhead. It proceeded, I believe, from the young mother,— the mother of the little one before spoken of. When the child had become restless before this, or when she was tired, a young man upon the brethren's side of the room had taken it for awhile, and now it was doubtless being put to sleep in a room overhead, into which a stove-pipe passed from the apartment where we sat.

My attention was also attracted by an old lady who sat near me, and facing the stove, with her hands crossed in her lap, and a gold* or brass ring on each middle finger. She wore a black flannel dress and a brown woolen apron, leather shoes and knit woolen stockings. Her head was bent forward toward her broad bosom, upon which was crossed a white kerchief. With her gray hair, round face, and plain linen cap, her whole figure reminded me of the peasant women of Continental Europe or of a Flemish picture.

When the long sermon was ended, different brethren were called upon, and during a half-hour we had from them several short discourses,

---

* "Were they not brass?" says one of my *Old Mennist* neighbors. "She wears them for some sickness, I reckon. She would not wear them for show. One of our preachers wears steel rings on his little fingers for cramps."

one or two of them nearly inaudible. The speakers were, I think, giving their views on what had been said, or perhaps they were by these little efforts preparing themselves to become preachers, or showing their gifts to the congregation.

It is stated in Herzog's Cyclopædia that among the Mennonites in Holland the number of Liebesprediger has greatly declined, so that some congregations had no preacher. (The word Liebesprediger I am inclined to translate as voluntary, unpaid preachers, like those among Friends.) I am in doubt, indeed, whether any such are now found in Holland. There seems to be no scarcity in this country of preachers, who are, however, in some, if not all three of the divisions of Mennonites, chosen by lot.

When these smaller efforts were over, the former preacher spoke again for twenty minutes, and several of the women were moved to tears. After this the congregation knelt in vocal prayer. When they rose, the preacher said that the next meeting would be at the house of John Lapp, in two weeks. He pronounced a benediction, ending with the name of Jesus, and the whole congregation, brethren and sisters, curtsied, or made a reverence, as the French express it. This was doubtless in allusion to the text, "At that name every knee shall bend." Finally, a hymn, or a portion of one, was sung, drawn out in a peculiar manner by dwelling on the words.

I obtained a hymn-book, and copied a portion. It seems obscure:

> "Der Schopfer auch der Vater heisst,
>   Durch Christum, seinen Sohne;
> Da wirket mit der Heilig Geist,
>   Einiger Gott drey Namen,
> Von welchem kommt ein Gotteskind
> Gewaschen ganz rein von der Sund,
>   Wird geistlich gespeisst und trancket,
> Mit Christi Blut, sein Willen thut
> Irdisch verschmacht aus ganzen Muthe,
> Der Vater sich ihm schenket."

The book from which I copied these lines was in large German print, and bore the date 1785. In front was this inscription, in the German tongue and handwriting: "This song-book belongs to me, Joseph B——. Written in the year of Christ 1791; and I received it from my father." Both father and son have been gathered to their fathers; the book, if I mistake not, was in the house of the grandson, and it may yet outlast several generations of these primitive people.

The services closed at a little after noon. From their having been conducted entirely in German, or in German and the dialect, some persons might suppose that these were recent immigrants to our country. But the B. family just alluded to was one of the first Amish families that came here, having arrived in 1737.

It seems that the language is cherished with care, as a means of preserving their religious and

other peculiarities. The public schools, however, which are almost entirely English, must
be a powerful means of assimilation.

The services being ended, the women quietly
busied themselves, while I wrote, in preparing
dinner. In a very short time two tables were
spread in the apartment where the meeting had
been held. Two tables, I have said,—and there
was one for the men to sit at,—but on the women's
side the *table* was formed of benches placed together, and, of course, was quite low. I should
have supposed that this was a casual occurrence,
had not an acquaintance told me that many years
ago, when she attended an Amish meeting, she
sat up to two benches.

Before eating there was a silent pause, during
which those men who had not yet a place at the
table stood uncovered reverentially, holding their
hats before their faces. In about fifteen minutes
the "first table" had finished eating, and another
silent pause was observed in the same manner
before they rose.

I was invited to the second table, where I
found beautiful white bread, butter, pies, pickles,
apple-butter, and refined molasses. I observed
that there were no spoons in the molasses and
apple-butter. A cup of coffee also was handed
to each person who wished it. We were not
invited to take more than one.

This meal marks the progress of wealth and

luxury, or the decline of asceticism, since the day when bean soup was the principal if not the only dish furnished on these occasions. The same neighbor who told me of sitting up to two benches many years ago, told me that at that time they were served with bean soup in bright dishes, doubtless of pewter or tin. Three or four persons ate out of one dish. It was very unhandy, she said.

But while thus sketching the manners of my simple, plain neighbors, let me not forget to acknowledge that ready hospitality which thus provides a comfortable meal even to strangers visiting the meeting. Besides myself, there were at least two others present who were not members,—two German Catholic women of the poorer class, such as hire out to work.

The silent pause before and after eating was also observed by the second table; and after we rose, a third company sat down.

When all were done, I gave a little assistance in clearing the tables, in carrying the butter into the cellar and the other food to the wash-house. The dishes were taken to the roofed porch between the latter and the house, where some of the women-folk washed them. A neat table stood at the foot of the cellar-stairs, and received the valued product of the dairy, the fragments being put away in an orderly manner.

I now had a time of leisure, for my driver had

7

gone to see a friend, and I must await his coming.   This gave me an opportunity to talk
with several sisters. I inquired of a fine-look-
ing woman when the feet-washing would be
held, and when they took the Lord's Supper.
When I asked whether they liked those who
were not members to attend the feet-washing,
I understood her to say that they did not. (I
attended, not a great while after, a great Whitsuntide feet-washing and Bread-breaking in the
meeting-house of the New Mennists.)

I had now an opportunity to examine the
books.   Standing upon a bench, I took down a
great volume, well printed in the German language, and entitled " The Bloody Theatre; or,
The Martyr's Mirror of the Baptists, or Defenceless Christians; who, on Account of the Testimony of Jesus, their Saviour, Suffered and were
Put to Death, from the Time of Christ to the Year
1660. Lancaster, 1814." This book was a version
from the Dutch (*Holländisch*) of Thielem J. van
Bracht, and it has also been rendered from
German into English. I was not aware, at the
time, that I had before me one of the principal
sources whence the history of the Mennonites is
to be drawn,—a history which is still unwritten.

The books were few in number, and I noticed
no other so remarkable as this. Another German
one, more modern in appearance, was entitled
" Universal Cattle-Doctor Book; or, The Cures

of the old Shepherd Thomas, of Bunzen, in Silesia, for Horses, Cattle, Sheep, Swine, and Goats."

While I was looking over the volumes, a little circumstance occurred, which, although not flattering to myself, is perhaps too characteristic to be omitted. My "Dutch" neighbors are not great readers, and to read German is considered an accomplishment even among those who speak the dialect. To speak "Dutch" is very common, of course, but to read German is a considerable attainment. I have, therefore, sometimes surprised a neighbor by being able to read the language. I am naturally not unwilling to be admired, and, as two or three sisters were standing near while I examined the books, I endeavored in haste to give them a specimen of my attainments. I therefore took a passage quickly from the great "Martyr-Book," and read aloud a sentence like this: "Grace, peace, and joy through God our Heavenly Father; wisdom, righteousness, and truth, through Jesus Christ his Son, together with the illumining of the Holy Spirit, be with you." Glancing up to see the surprise which my attainments must produce, I beheld a different expression of countenance, for the attention of some of the thoughtful sisters was attracted by the subject-matter, instead of the reader, and that aroused a sentiment of devotion beautifully expressed.

I asked our host, " Have you no history of your society ?"

" No," he answered; " we just hand it down."

I have since heard, however, that there are papers or written records in charge of a person who lives at some distance from me. From certain printed records I have been able to trace a streamlet of history from its source in Switzerland, where the Anabaptists suffered persecution in Berne, Zurich, etc. I have read of their exile in Alsace and the Palatinate; of the aid afforded to them by their fellow-believers, the Mennonites of Holland; and of their final colonization in Pennsylvania, where they also are called Mennists.

Nearly all the congregation had departed when my driver at last arrived. I shook hands with those that were left, and kissed the pleasant old lady, the mother of our host.

SWISS EXILES.

THE plain people among whom I live, Quaker-like in appearance, and, like the Quakers, opposed to oaths and to war,* are in a great measure descendants of Swiss Baptists or Anabaptists, who were banished from their country for refusing to conform to the established Reformed Church.

Some of the early exiles took refuge in Alsace and the Palatinate, and afterwards came to Pennsylvania, settling in Lancaster County, under the kind patronage of our distinguished first Proprietor. William Penn's sympathy for them was doubtless increased by their so much resembling himself in many important particulars.

If any one inclines to investigate the tradi-

---

* Our German Baptists are more non-resistant than the Quakers. Some of them refuse to vote for civil officers.

The term Anabaptist is from the Greek, and signifies one who baptizes again. All Baptists baptize anew those who were baptized in infancy. The term Anabaptist, in the present essay, is used indiscriminately with Baptist, and, in a degree, with Mennonite.

tions of these people, let him ask the plain old men of the county whence they originated. I think that a great part of the Amish and other Mennonites will tell him of their Swiss origin.

Nor are very important written records wanting upon the subject of the Swiss persecutions. Two volumes in use among our German Baptists narrate the story.

The first is the great Martyr-book, called " The Bloody Theatre; or Martyr's Mirror of the Defenceless Christians," by Thielem J. van Bracht, published in Dutch, about the year 1660, translated into German, and afterwards into English.*

The second printed record, circulating in our county, and describing the sufferings of some of the Swiss Anabaptists, is a hymn-book formerly in use among our "old Mennists," but now, I think, employed only by the Amish.

It is a collection of "several beautiful Christian songs," composed in prison at Bassau,† in the castle, by the Switzer Brethren, "and by other orthodox (*rechtglaubige*) Christians, here and there."

I know of no English version.

Near the close of this hymn-book there is an account of the afflictions which were endured by

---

* The English version is one of the labors of Daniel Rupp.

† Bassau is, I suppose, upon the Danube, in Bavaria. Is it not written *Passau* in the Martyr-book?

the brethren in Switzerland, in the canton of Zurich, on account of the gospel ("um des Evangeliums willen").

The first-mentioned work, the great Martyr-book, is a ponderous volume.

The author begins his martyrology with Jesus, John, and Stephen, whom he includes among the Baptist or the defenceless martyrs. I suppose that he includes them among the Baptists on the ground that they were not baptized in infancy, but upon faith. From these, the great story comes down in one thousand octavo pages, describing the intense cruelties of the Roman emperors, telling of persecutions by the Saracens, persecutions of the Waldenses and Albigenses, and describing especially the sufferings which the Baptists (in common with other Protestants) endured in Holland under the reigns of Charles V. and Philip II.*

The narrative of the persecution of the Anabaptists of Switzerland by their fellow-Protestants is mostly found at the close of the volume. It comes down to the year 1672, and may be, in part at least, an appendix to the original volume.

Allusions to the severe treatment of the Ana-

---

* Of the heretics executed by Alva in the Spanish Netherlands, a large proportion were Anabaptists.—*Encyclopædia Americana.*

baptists of Switzerland may also be found in Herzog's and in Appleton's Cyclopædia.

In the former work, we read that Anabaptism, after a public theological disputation, was by the help of the authorities suppressed in Switzerland.*

In the American Cyclopædia (article Anabaptists), we read that Melanchthon and Zwingli were themselves troubled by questions respecting infant baptism, in connection with the personal faith required by Protestantism. Nevertheless, Zwingli himself is said to have pronounced sentence upon Mentz, who had been his friend and fellow-student, in these words: "Whosoever dips (or baptizes) a second time, let him be dipped." "Qui iterum mergit, mergatur." This humorous saying appears to be explained in the Martyr-book, where we read that Felix Mentz was drowned at Zurich "for the truth of the gospel," in 1526. The persecution of such men is said to have shocked the moderate of all parties.

Upon the authority of Balthazar Hubmor (whom I suppose to be the Hubmeyer of the Cyclopædia), the Martyr-book states that Zuin-

---

* How thoroughly it was suppressed may be inferred from the fact that of the population of Berne, in 1850, only one thousand persons are put down as Baptists in a population of 458,000. Of the remainder, 54,000 are Catholics, and the remainder of the Reformed Church (I give round numbers).— See the American Cyclopædia.

glius, etc., imprisoned at one time twenty persons of both sexes, in a dark tower, never more to see the light of the sun.

This earliest Swiss Protestant persecution occurred, it will be observed, about 1526, and the latest recorded in the Martyr-book, in or about 1672, covering a period of nearly one hundred and fifty years.*

At the same time that the Swiss Baptists were suffering at the hands of other Protestants, Anabaptists of the peaceful class were found in Holland in large numbers. The record of their sufferings and martyrs (says the American Cyclopædia) furnishes a touching picture in human history. William of Orange, founder of the Dutch republic, was sustained in the gloomiest hours by their sympathy and aid.† That great prince, however importuned, steadily refused to persecute them.

Simon Menno, born at the close of the fifteenth or the commencement of the sixteenth century, educated for the priesthood of the Roman Catholic Church, converted in manhood to the faith of the Anabaptists, became their chief leader.

---

* Zschokke, in his History of Switzerland, accuses the Anabaptists of causing great trouble and scandal. Some account of the furious or warlike Anabaptists of Holland may be found in the American Cyclopædia.

† This must not be understood as aid in bearing arms.

Mennonites and Anabaptists have from his time been interchangeable terms.*

It was about seventeen years after the drowning of Mentz in Switzerland, and while the Catholic persecution was raging in Holland, that in the year 1543 an imperial edict was issued

---

* One of Menno's brothers is said to have been connected with the Anabaptists of Münster, those who took up arms, etc. Of these, whose course was so very different from the lives of our defenceless Baptists in this country, Menno may have obtained some, after their defeat, to come under the peaceable rule. There are in the Netherlands, says a recent authority, 40,000 Mennonites. They are a true, pure Netherlandish appearance, which is older than the Reformation, and therefore must not be identified with the Protestantism of the sixteenth century.

Menno Simon does not mert to be called the father of the Netherlandish Mennonites, but rather the first shepherd of the scattered sheep,—the founder of their church community.

The ground-thought from which Menno proceeded was not, as with Luther, justification by faith, or, as with the Swiss Reformers, the absolute dependence of the sinner upon God, in the work of salvation. The holy Christian life, in opposition to worldliness, was the point whence Menno proceeded, and to which he always returned. In the Romish Church we see ruling the spirit of Peter; in the Reformed Evangelical, the spirit of Paul; in Menno we see arise again, James the Just, the brother of the Lord.

See articles *Menno* and the *Mennonites*, and *Holland*, in Herzog's "Real-Encyclopädie," Stuttgart and Hamburg, 1858. Many of the Mennonites of Holland at the present day seem to have wandered far from the teachings of Menno, and to be very different from the simple Mennonite communities of Pennsylvania.

against Menno; for both parties persecuted the
Baptists,—the Catholics in the Low Countries,
the Protestants in Switzerland. The Martyr-book
tells us that a dreadful decree was proclaimed
through all West Friesland, containing an offer
of general pardon, the favor of the emperor, and
a hundred carlgulden to all malefactors and murderers who would deliver Menno Simon into the
hands of the executioners. Under pain of death,
it was forbidden to harbor him; but God preserved and protected him wonderfully, and he
died a natural death, near Lubeck, in the open
field, in 1559, aged sixty-six.

It is further mentioned that he was buried in
his own garden.*

About fourteen years after the death of Menno,
or in the year 1573, we read in the Martyr-book
that Dordrecht had submitted to the reigning
prince, William of Orange, the first not to shed
blood on account of faith or belief.

But the toleration which William extended to
the Baptists was not imitated by his great com-
peer, Elizabeth of England. For the Martyr-
book tells us that in 1575, " some friends," who

---

* The burying of Menno in his own garden can be explained by the great secrecy which in times of persecution
attended the actions of the persecuted sects. The family
graveyards of Lancaster County, located upon farms, may be
in some degree traditional from times of persecution, when
Baptists had no churches, etc., but met in secret.

had fled to England, having met in the suburbs of London "to hear the word of God," were spied out, and the constable took them to prison. Two of these were burnt at Smithfield, in the eighteenth year of Elizabeth. Jan Pieters was one of them, a poor man whose first wife had been burnt at Ghent. He then married a second, whose first husband had been burnt at the same place.

Thus it befell the unfortunate Jan that while his wife was burnt by Catholics, he himself suffered at the hands of English Protestants.*

The expression "sheep" or "lambs," which is applied to some of the Baptist martyrs, alludes, I suppose, to their non-resistance. Thus, in 1576, Hans Bret, a servant, whose master was about to be apprehended, gave him warning, so that he escaped, but himself, "this innocent follower of Christ, fell into the paws of the wolves.". . . . . "As he stood at the stake, they kindled the fire, and burnt this sheep alive."

The next year after this, William of Orange had occasion to call to order, as it appears, some of his own subjects. The magistrates of Middelburg had announced to the Baptists that they must take an oath of fidelity and arm themselves, or else give up their business and shut up their houses.

---

* To the writer it is a question of some interest how far George Fox, the founder of Quakerism, was acquainted with the lives, sufferings, and writings of the Anabaptists.

The Baptists had recourse to William, promising to pay levies and taxes, and desiring to be believed on their yea and nay. William granted their request, their yea was to be taken in the place of an oath, and the delinquent was to be punished as for perjury.

In William Penn's Treatise on Oaths, it is stated that William of Orange said, "Those men's yea must pass for an oath, and we must not urge this thing any further, or we must confess that the Papists had reason to force us to a religion that was against our conscience."

About nine years after William had thus reproved the magistrates of Middelburg, or in the year 1586, the Baptists came to grief elsewhere. It is stated that those called Anabaptists, who had taken refuge in the Prussian dominions, were ordered by "the prince of the country" to depart from his entire Duchy of Prussia, and in the next year from all his dominions. This was because they were said to speak scandalously of infant baptism.

About the close of the century, pleasanter times for the Baptists seem to have followed. "When the north wind of persecution became violent, there were intervals when the pleasant south wind of liberty and repose succeeded."

"But now occurred the greatest mischief in Zurich and Berne, by those who styled themselved Reformed;" but others of the same name,

" especially the excellent regents of the United Netherlands," opposed such proceedings.

The Martyr-book says, in substance, "It is a lamentable case that those who boast that they are the followers of the defenceless Lamb, do no longer possess the lamb's disposition, but, on the contrary, have the nature of the wolf. It seems as if they could not bear it that any should travel towards heaven in any other way than that which they go themselves, as was exemplified in the case of Hans Landis, who was a minister and teacher of the gospel of Christ. Being taken to Zurich, he refused to desist from preaching and to deny his faith, and was sentenced to death,— the edict of eighty years before not having died of old age. They, however, persuaded the common people that he was not put to death for religion's sake, but for disobedience to the authorities."*

After the death of Hans Landis, persecution

---

* Hans (or John) Landis is the name of the sufferer just spoken of. Several Landises are mentioned in the Martyr ologies, and the name is very common in Lancaster County at this time. John Landis is remarkably so.

In quoting from the Martyr-book, I employ the English version, "Martyr's Mirror." I have lately had an opportunity of seeing an old German copy, from the press of the Brotherhood at Ephrata, about 1750. I find that it is differently arranged from the modern English version, and suspect other variations.

rested for twenty-one years, when the ancient hatred broke out afresh in Zurich.

The Baptists now asked permission to leave the country with their property, but this was not granted to them. " They might choose," says the Martyrology, "to go with them [the Reformed] to church, or to die in prison. To the first they would not consent; therefore they might expect the second."

This brings us to the era of the persecution described in the Hymn-book of which I formerly spoke,—the book now in use among the Amish of our county.

This little volume—little when compared to the ponderous Martyr-book—gives an account of the persecution in Zurich between the years 1635 and 1645. Many of the persons mentioned in the Hymn-book as suffering at this time appear to be of families now found in Lancaster County,—not only from the Hymn-book's being preserved here, but especially because the surnames are the same as are now found here, or are slightly different. Thus, we have Landis, Meylin, Strickler, Bachmann, and Gut, now Good; Müller, now Miller; Baumann, now Bowman.

Mention is made of about eighteen persons who died in prison during this persecution, in the period of nine or ten years. Proclamation was made from the pulpits forbidding the people to afford shelter to the Baptists: even their own

children who harbored them were liable to be
fined,—as Hans Müller's wife and children, who
were fined forty pounds because "they showed
mercy to their dear father."

The Hymn-book states that the Gelehrte (the
learned?) accompanied the captors, running day
and night with their servants. Many fell into
the power of the authorities,—man and woman,
the pregnant, the nursing mother, the sick.

In the midst of this persecution, the authorities of Amsterdam, themselves Calvinists or
Reformed, being moved by the solicitations of
the Baptists of Amsterdam, sent a respectful
petition to the burgomaster and council of
Zurich, to mitigate the persecution; but the
petition, it is said, excited an unfriendly and
irritating answer.

It seems that some of the Baptists, harassed
in Zurich, took refuge in Berne; and about the
time that the persecution in Zurich came to a
close, or about 1645, it is stated that "those of
Berne" threatened the Baptists. About four
years after, "those of Schaffhausen" issued an
edict against the people called Anabaptists.*

Only a few years later, or in 1653, as we read
in the Martyr-book, there was another perse-

---

* From Schaffhausen came some of the Stauffer family, as
I have read. The Stauffers are numerous in our county. For
some family traditions, see "The Dunker Love-Feast."

cution elsewhere. The record says, in substance, "As a lamb in making its escape from
the wolf is eventually seized by the bear" (we
like the quaint language), "so it obtained for
several defenceless followers of the meek Jesus,
who, persecuted in Switzerland by the Zwing-
lians, were permitted to live awhile in peace in
the Alpine districts, under a Roman Catholic
prince, Willem Wolfgang. About this year,
however, this prince banished the Anabaptists,
so called. But they were received in peace and
with joy elsewhere, particularly in Cleves,*
under the Elector of Brandenburg, and in the
Netherlands. 'When they persecute you in
one city,' saith the Lord, 'flee ye into another.'"

About six years after, or in 1659, an edict
was issued in Berne, of which extracts are given
in the Martyr-book. If the edict in full brings
no more serious charges against the Baptists
than do these extracts, this paper itself may be
regarded as a noble vindication of the Anabaptists of Switzerland at this era.

According to the substance of this Bernese
edict, the teachers of this people—*i.e.* the preach-

---

* In the duchy of Cleves, the town of Crefeld, some fifty
or sixty years later, gave refuge to the Dunkers. It appears
also to have harbored some of the French Protestants who
fled from their country on the revocation of the Edict of
Nantes. See "Ephrata."

8*

ers—were to be seized wherever they could be
sought out, " and brought to our Orphan Asylum
to receive the treatment necessary to their con-
version; or, if they persist in their obstinacy, they
are to receive the punishment in such cases belonging. Meantime the officers are to seize
their property, and present an inventory of the
same.

" To the Baptists in general, who refuse to desist from their error, the punishment of exile
shall be announced. It is our will and command that they be escorted to the borders, a
solemn promise obtained from them, since they
will not swear, and that they be banished entirely from our country till it be proved that
they have been converted. Returning uncon-
verted, and refusing to recant, they shall be
whipped, branded, and again banished, which
condign punishment is founded upon the following reasons and motives:

" 1. All subjects should confirm with an oath
the allegiance which they owe to the authorities
ordained them of God. The Anabaptists, who
refuse the oath, cannot be tolerated.

" 2. Subjects should acknowledge that the magistracy is from God, and with God. But the
Anabaptists, who declare that the magisterial
office cannot exist in the Christian Church, are
not to be tolerated in the country.

" 3. All subjects are bound to protect and defend their country. But the Anabaptists refuse to bear arms, and cannot be tolerated. . . .

"5. The magistracy is ordained of God, to punish evil-doers, especially murderers, etc. But the Anabaptists refuse to report these to the authorities, and therefore they cannot be tolerated.

"6. Those who refuse to submit to the wholesome ordinances of the government, and who act in opposition to it, cannot be tolerated. Now, the Anabaptists transgress in the following manner:

"They preach without the calling of the magistracy; baptize without the command of the authorities; . . . . and do not attend the meetings of the church.

"We have unanimously resolved that all should inflict banishment and the other penalties against all who belong to this corrupted and extremely dangerous and wicked sect, that they may make no further progress, but that the country may be freed from them; on which, in grace, we rely.

"As regards the estate of the disobedient exiles, or of those who have run away, it shall, after deducting costs, be divided among the wives and children who remain in obedience.

"We command that no person shall lodge nor give dwelling to a Baptist, whether related to him or not, nor afford him the necessaries of life. But every one of our persuasion should be exhorted to report whatever information he can obtain of them to the high bailiff.

"And an especial proclamation of this last article shall be made from the pulpit."

This Bernese edict, being read in all parts, was a source of great distress, and it appeared to the Baptists as if " the beautiful flower of the orthodox Christian Church" would be entirely extirpated in those parts.

It was therefore concluded to send certain persons from the cities of Dordrecht, Leyden, Amsterdam, etc., to the Hague, where the puissant States-General were in session, to induce them to send petitions to Berne and Zurich for the relief of the people suffering oppression.

The States-General, as "kind fathers of the poor, the miserable, and the oppressed," took immediate cognizance of the matter.

Letters were written " to the lords of Berne" for the liberation of prisoners, etc., and to the lords of Zurich for the restoration of the property of the imprisoned, deceased, and exiled Baptists. The letter to Berne narrates (in brief) that " the States-General have learned from persons called in this country Mennonists, that their brethren called Anabaptists suffer great persecution at Berne, being forbidden to live in the country, but not allowed to remove with their families and property. We have likewise learned that some of them have been closely confined; which has moved us to Christian compassion.

"We request you, after the good example of the lords-regent of Schaffhausen, to grant the petitioners time to depart with their families and property wherever they choose. To this end, we request you to consider that when, in 1655, the Waldenses were so virulently persecuted by the Romans for the confession of their reformed religion, and the necessities of the dispersed people could not be relieved but by large collections raised in England, this country, etc., the churches of the Baptists, upon the simple recommendation of their governments, and in Christian love and compassion, contributed with so much benevolence that a remarkably large sum was raised. . . . . Farewell, etc. At the Hague, 1660."

The letter of the States-General to Zurich is similar to the foregoing abstract.

Besides these acts of the States-General, several cities of the United Netherlands, being entirely opposed to restraint of conscience, reproved "the members of their society in Switzerland," and exhorted them to gentleness.

Thus, the burgomasters and lords of Rotterdam, speaking in behalf of the elders of the church called Mennonist, whose fellow-believers in Berne are called in derision Anabaptists: "As to ourselves, honorable lords, we are of opinion that

these men can be safely tolerated in the common-
wealth, and for this judgment we have to thank
William, Prince of Orange, of blessed memory,
who established, by his bravery, liberty of conscience for us, and could never be induced to
deprive the Mennonites of citizenship.

" We have never repented of this, for we have
never learned that these people have sought to
excite sedition, but, on the contrary, they have
cheerfully paid their taxes.

" Although they confess that Christians cannot
conscientiously act as officers of government, and
are opposed to swearing, yet they do not refuse
obedience to the authorities, and, if they are con-
victed of a violation of truth, are willing to un-
dergo the punishment due to perjury. We indulge
the hope that your lordships will either repeal
the onerous decree against the Mennonists, or at
least grant to the poor wanderers sufficient time
to make their preparations, and procure residences in other places.

" When this is done, your lordships will have
accomplished a measure well pleasing to God,
advantageous to the name of the Reformed, and
gratifying to us who are connected with your
lordships in the close ties of religion. Rotterdam, 1660."*

---

* Abstracted from the passage or letter in the great Baptist
Martyr-book, the " Martyr's Mirror."

These appeals of the States-General and of the cities of Holland seem to have had very little effect, at least upon the authorities of Berne, for there arose eleven years later, or in 1671, another severe persecution of the Baptists in that canton, which was so virulent that it seemed as if the authorities would not cease until they had expelled that people entirely.

In consequence of this, seven hundred persons, old and young, were constrained to forsake their property, relations, and country, and retire to the Palatinate.* Some, it seems, took refuge in Alsace, above Strasburg.

An extract from a letter given in the Martyr-book says, "Some follow chopping wood, others labor in the vineyards; hoping, I suppose, that after some time tranquillity will be restored, and they will be able to return to their habitations; but I am afraid that this will not happen soon. . . . The authorities of Berne had six of the prisoners (one of whom was a man that had nine children) put in chains and sold as galley-slaves between Milan and Malta."†

---

* " Martyr's Mirror."

† This, it appears, is not the first instance of this punishment being inflicted at Berne. A list in the Martyr-book of persons put to death for their faith concludes thus: "Copied from the letter of Hans Loersch, while in prison at Berne, 1667, whence he was taken in chains to sea."

The dreadful fate of the galley-slave who was chained to the oar or to the bench, exposed to the society of criminals,

This severe penalty of being sold as slaves to row the galleys or great sail-boats which traversed the Mediterranean, was also impending over other able-bodied prisoners, as it is said, but "a lord of Berne," named Beatus, was excited to compassion, and obtained permission that the prisoners should leave the country upon bail that they would not return without permission.

In the year 1672, the brethren in the United Netherlands (the Mennonites or Baptists) sent some of their members into the Palatinate to inquire into the condition of the refugees, and the latter were comforted and supported by the assistance of the churches and members of the United Netherlands.

There were among the refugees husbands and wives who had to abandon their consorts, who belonged to the Reformed Church and could not think of removal.

Among these were two ministers, whose families did not belong to the church (Baptist), and who had to leave without finding whether their wives would go with them, or whether they loved their property more than their husbands. "Such incidents occasioned the greater distress, since the authorities granted such persons remaining permission to marry again."*

---

etc., may be found alluded to in works of fiction, such as Zschokke's "Alamontade, or the Galley-Slave."

* "Martyr's Mirror."

Alsace and the Palatinate (lying upon the Rhine), where our Swiss exiles had taken refuge, were soon after devastated in the great wars of their ambitious neighbor, Louis XIV., King of France. Turenne, the French general, put the Palatinate, a fine and fertile country, full of populous towns and villages, to fire and sword. The Elector Palatine, from the top of his castle at Manheim, beheld two cities and twenty towns in flames.*

Turenne, with the same indifference, destroyed the ovens, and laid waste part of the country of Alsace, to prevent the enemy from subsisting.†

About fourteen years after, or in the winter of 1688–9, the Palatinate was again ravaged by the French king's army. The French generals gave notice to the towns but lately repaired, and then so flourishing, to the villages, etc., that their inhabitants must quit their dwellings, although it was then the dead of winter; for all was to be destroyed by fire and sword.

"The flames with which Turenne had destroyed two towns and twenty villages of the Palatinate were but sparks in comparison to this last terrible destruction, which all Europe looked upon with horror."‡

---

* Voltaire's "Age of Louis XIV."

† The troops of the Empire of Germany, or of Germany and Spain combined. See "Age of Louis XIV."

‡ Ibid.

Between the time of these two great raids there occurred several noteworthy incidents. There came to Holland and Germany, in the year 1677, a man who was then of little note, a man of peace, belonging to a new and persecuted sect, but who has since become better known in history, at least to us who inhabit Pennsylvania, than Marshal Turenne, or the great Louis XIV. himself. It was the colonist and statesman, the Quaker, William Penn.

The Elector Palatine now reigning was a relative of the King of England. Penn failed to see this prince, but he addressed a letter to him, to the "Prince Elector Palatine of Heydelbergh," in which he desires to know "what encouragement a colony of virtuous and industrious families might hope to receive from thee, in case they should transplant themselves into this country, which certainly in itself is very excellent, respecting taxes, oaths, arms, etc."*

I know not what encouragement, if any, the Elector offered to Penn; but only about four years later, Penn's great colony was founded

---

* Several towns and townships in southeastern Pennsylvania bear record of the Palatinate, etc. In Lancaster County we have Strasburg, doubtless named for that city in Alsace, and two Manheims. Adjoining counties have Heidelbergs. The Swiss Palatines do not seem to have preserved enough affection for the land of their origin to bestow Swiss names upon our Lancaster County towns. What wonder?

across the Atlantic, a colony which afforded refuge to many "Palatines."

Of this journey to Germany and Holland, just spoken of, Penn kept a journal, and there is mention made at Amsterdam of Baptists and "Menists," or Mennonites; but whether he ever met in Europe any of our Swiss exiles, I do not find stated in history. Of his other two journeys to Germany, no journal has been found.

Eight years after Penn's journey, there occurred, in the year 1685, two circumstances which may have especially interested our Swiss Baptists and have operated to bring their colony to Pennsylvania.

"In June, 1685, the Elector Palatine dying without issue, the electoral dignity went to a bigoted Popish family. In October, the King of France recalled the Edict of Nantes."* Five or six hundred thousand Frenchmen are said to have left their country at the time of this cruel act, and the Palatinate doubtless received many of the wanderers.†

The Swiss exiles that first took refuge in Lancaster County came here about thirty-eight years after the severe Bernese persecution of 1671.

---

* The above I have found credited to Bishop Burnet.

† If so, it does not appear to have furnished a safe resting-place. Six thousand distressed Palatines, it is said, sought refuge in England under the patronage of Queen Anne.

Rupp, the historian of our county, tells us that in 1706 or 1707 a number of the persecuted Swiss Mennonites went to England and made a particular agreement with the honorable proprietor, William Penn, for lands.

He further says that several families from the Palatinate, descendants of the distressed Swiss, emigrated to America and settled in Lancaster County in the year 1709.*

The next year, the commissioners of property had agreed with Martin Kendig, Hans Herr, etc., Swissers lately arrived in this province, for ten thousand acres of land, twenty miles east of Connystogoe.†

The supplies of the colonists were at first scanty, until the seed sown in a fertile soil yielded some thirty-, others forty-fold.‡ Their nearest mill was at Wilmington, distant, as I estimate, about thirty miles.

One of their number was soon sent to Europe to bring out other emigrants, and after the accession the colony numbered about thirty fami-

---

* This was twenty-eight years after the founding of Penn's colony. Several years earlier, or in 1701, some Mennonites bought land in Germantown, and in 1708 built a church (or meeting-house). For this information I am obliged to Dr. Oswald Seidensticker.

† The above-mentioned "Connystogoe" it would probably be very difficult to point out. The Conestoga Creek empties into the Susquehanna below Lancaster.

‡ Rupp.

lies. They mingled with the Indians in hunting
and fishing. These were hospitable and respectful to the whites.*

We are told that the early colonists had strong
faith in the fruitfulness and natural advantages
of their choice of lands. "They knew these
would prove to them and their children the home
of plenty." Their anticipations have never failed.†

The harmony existing between the Indians
and these men of peace is very pleasing. Soon
after their first settlement here, Lieutenant-
Governor Gookin made a journey to Conestogo (1711), and in a speech to the Indians tells
them that Governor Penn intends to present five
belts of wampum to the Five Nations, "and one
to you of Conestogo, and requires your friend-
ship to the Palatines, settled near Pequea."‡

---

* Rupp.

† The question has been discussed, why did the Germans
select the limestone lands, and the Scotch-Irish take those less
fruitful? Different hints upon this subject may be found in
Day's Historical Collections of Pennsylvania. Under the
head of Lancaster County, he says that a number of Scotch-
Irish, in consequence of the limestone land being liable to
frost and heavily wooded, seated themselves (1763) along the
northern line of the counties of Chester and Lancaster.

A gentleman of Marietta, in this county, has said to me
nearly as follows: "Ninety in one hundred of the regular
members of the Mennonite churches are farmers, and they
follow the limestone land as the needle follows the pole."

‡ The Pequea Creek (pronounced by the "Dutch" Peck'-

About seven years after this, William Penn died in England, in the year 1718.

Whether the persecution of the Baptists continued in Switzerland, and had begun in the Palatinate, I am not able to say, further than to offer the following passage, taken from Herzog's Cyclopædia:

"When the Baptists were oppressed in Switzerland and the Palatinate, the Mennonites united into one community with the Palatines, at Groningen (Holland), and established in 1726 a fund for the needy abroad, to which Baptists of all parties richly contributed. About eighty years after, this fund was discontinued, being no longer thought necessary."

Thus active persecution of the Baptists in those regions had ceased, as it seems, about the year 1800.

The German or Swiss colony in Lancaster County is said to have caused some alarm, though we can hardly believe it a real fear. Nine years after the death of William Penn, representation was made to Lieutenant-Governor Gordon (1727) that " a large number of Germans, peculiar in their dress, religion, and notions of political government, had settled on Pequea, and were determined not to obey the lawful authority of

---

way) waters some of the finest land in the county, or the very finest. "The Piquaws had their wigwams scattered along the banks of the Pequea."

government; that they had resolved to speak their own language, and to acknowledge no sovereign but the great Creator of the universe."

Rupp, from whom I quote the above passage, adds, "There was perhaps never a people who felt less disposed to disobey the lawful authority of government than the Mennonites, against whom these charges were made."

The charges were doubtless dropped, or answered in a satisfactory manner; for two years subsequently, or in 1729, a naturalization act was passed concerning certain Germans who had come into the province between the years 1700 and 1718.

Over one hundred persons are naturalized by this act (Martin Meylin, Hans Graaf, etc.); and a great part of the people of the county can find their surnames mentioned therein.*

All the names, however, are not those of Baptist families.

Nearly to the same date as this naturalization

---

* Not always as at present spelled. The present Kendig appears as Kindeck, Breneman as Preniman, Baumgardner as Bumgarner, Eby as Abye. These were probably English efforts at spelling German names. Rupp says that he was indebted to Abraham Meylin, of West Lampeter Township, for a copy of the act. There appear to have been among the Palatines who came into our county some Huguenot families; but, from intermarrying with the Germans, and speaking the dialect, they are considered "Dutch." The name of the Bushong family is said to have once been Beauchamp.

act belongs a letter written from Philadelphia, in 1730, by the Rev. Jedediah Andrews.

Mr. Andrews says, in substance, "There are in this province a vast number of Palatines; those that have come of late years are mostly Reformed. The first-comers, though called Palatines, are mostly Switzers, many of whom are wealthy, having got the best land in the province. They live sixty or seventy miles off, but come frequently to town with their wagons laden with skins belonging to the Indian traders, with butter, flour, etc."*

Mr. Andrews, in his letter, while speaking of the Switzers, continues:

"There are many Lutherans and some Reformed mixed among them. . . . Though there be so many sorts of religion going on, we don't quarrel about it. We not only live peaceably, but seem to love one another."

This harmony among the multitudinous sects in Pennsylvania must have been the more remarkable to Mr. Andrews, from his having been born and educated in Massachusetts, where a very different state of affairs had prevailed.

---

* This mention of the Switzers' wagons reminds me of the great Conestoga wagons, which, before the construction of railroads, conveyed the produce of the interior to Philadelphia. With their long bodies roofed with white canvas, they went along almost, I might say, like moving houses. They were drawn by six powerful horses, at times furnished with trappings and bells; and the wagoner's trade was one of importance.

On this subject Rupp says, " The descendants of the Puritans boast that their ancestors fled from persecution, willing to encounter perils in the wilderness, and perils by the heathen, rather than be deprived of the free exercise of their religion.

" The descendants of the Swiss Mennonites in Lancaster County claim that while their ancestors sought for the same liberty, they did not persecute others who differed from them in religious opinion."*

The letter of Mr. Andrews, lately quoted, bears date 1730. Twelve years after, or in 1742, a respectable number of the Amish (pronounced Ommish) of Lancaster County petitioned the General Assembly that a special law of naturalization might be passed for their benefit. They stated that they had emigrated from Europe by an invitation from the proprietaries; that they had been brought up in and were attached to the Amish doctrine; and were conscientiously scrupulous against taking oaths ; " they therefore cannot be naturalized agreeably to the existing law." An act was passed in conformity to their request.

---

* A test-oath, or oath of abjuration, seems to have been in force at one time in Pennsylvania, concerning the Roman Catholics. (See Rupp's History of Berks and Lebanon.) Must we not attribute this act to the Royal Home government rather than to William Penn ?

(I give this statement as I find it, although some-what surprised if the laws of Pennsylvania did not always allow those to affirm who were conscientiously opposed to oaths.)

The history of our Swiss Exiles is nearly finished. It is chiefly when a nation is in adversity that its history is interesting to us. What is there to tell of a well-to-do farming population, who do not participate in battles, and who live almost entirely secluded from public affairs?

Under the date 1754, it is noted that Governor Pownall, traveling in Lancaster County, says, "I saw the finest farm one can possibly conceive, in the highest culture; it belongs to a Switzer." Thus Gray's lines (slightly altered) may be said to comprise most of the external history of these people for a century and a half:

> Oft did the harvest to their sickle yield,
>   Their furrow oft the stubborn glebe hath broke;
> How early did they drive their team a-field,
>   How bowed the woods beneath their sturdy stroke!

Some difficulty had arisen, however, between the Germans of our county and the "Scotch-Irish." Thus, Day, in his Historical Collections, says, "The Presbyterians from the north of Ireland came in at about the same time with the Germans, and occupied the townships of Donegal and Paxton." (Paxton, now Dauphin

County.) " Collisions afterwards occurring between them and the Germans, concerning elections, bearing of arms, the treatment of the
Indians, etc., the proprietaries instructed their
agents in 1755 that the Germans should be en-
couraged, and in a manner directed to settle
along the southern boundary of the province, in
Lancaster and York Counties, while the Irish
were to be located nearer to the Kittatinny
Mountain, in the region now forming Dauphin
and Cumberland Counties.*

In the Revolutionary War, the German Mennonites did not early espouse the cause of independence. Some of them doubtless felt bound by
their promise of loyalty to the established government, while others were perhaps influenced
by the motive lately attributed to them in the
correspondence of one of our county papers (" Ex-
aminer and Herald," Lancaster, October 27th,
1869). The writer tells us that Lancaster County
was settled principally by Mennonites, etc., who
are strict non-resistants. They were peculiarly
solicitous to manifest their loyalty to the powers
that be, because they had been accused by their

---

* It was not long after this date (in 1763) that the "Paxton Boys" made a raid down to Lancaster and massacred
the remnant of Conestoga Indians, in the jail of that town.

Day says that there was policy in the order above given;
that the Irish were warlike, and could defend the frontier.

enemies of having been implicated in rebellion during the unhappy events at Münster, Germany, in the years 1635–36.

When our Revolutionary struggle began, these people were cautious in resisting the established government.

During the late rebellion, although very few of our German Baptists bore arms, yet some, I think, were active in raising funds to pay bounties to persons who did enlist.

It appears to the writer that there can scarcely be a people in our country among whom the ancient practices are more faithfully maintained than among the Amish of Lancaster County.*

In the great falling off from ancient principles and practices which we read of among Holland Mennonites (see Herzog's Cyclopædia and the Encyclopædia Americana), it seems that there are yet left in Europe others of the stricter rule.

In Friesland, Holland, where the Mennonites are divided, as here, into three classes, there are found, by comparison, most traces of the old Mennonism. (See Herzog.)

---

* The Amish seem to have originated in Europe, about the year 1700, when Jacob Amen, a Swiss preacher, set up, or returned to, the more severe rule, distasteful to brethren in Alsace, etc., and enforced the ban of excommunication upon some or all of those who disagreed with him.

A small pamphlet upon this subject has been published at Elkhart, Indiana, and is for sale at the office of the *Herald of Truth.*

And we have lately heard of Amish in France.
A letter from that country, published in the
Herald of Truth (Elkhart, Indiana, July, 1871)
alludes to the late European war. The writer
says, " The loss we here sustained is indescrib-
able. Many houses have been entirely shattered
to pieces by the cannon-balls, and others totally
destroyed by fire." He adds, " As you desire to
know what kind of Mennonites there are residing
here in France, I will briefly state that most of
them are Amish Mennonites." He signs himself Isaac Rich, Etupes, par Audincourt, Doubs,
France. This locality, as I understand, is not
far from Switzerland and Alsace.

The church history of our Mennonites has not
been entirely uneventful.

Rupp tells us that they were very numerous
about the year 1792, and that Martin Boehm and
others made inroads upon them. A considerable
number seceded and joined the United Brethren,
or Vereinigte Brüder.

A society of Dunkers was formed near the
Susquehanna, many years ago, by Jacob Engle,
who had been a Mennonite. This society is
called " The River Brethren," and from it has
been formed the " Brinser Brethren," popularly
so called.

The Rev. John Herr is generally considered
the founder of a sect popularly called " New
Mennists." They call themselves, however,

10

"Reformed Mennonites," and claim that they have only returned to the ancient purity of doctrine.

How far the "Albrechtsleut," or "Dutch Methodists,"—the Evangelical Association, as they call themselves,—have made converts among the Mennonites, I cannot tell.

Mr. Rupp, whose History of Lancaster County is as yet the standard, speaks of the Mennonites as the prevailing religious denomination in 1843, having about forty-five ministers preaching in German, and over thirty-five meeting-houses.

The Amish meet in private houses.

Although I have never heard that our Mennonites as a religious body passed any rules forbidding slaveholding, as did the Quakers, yet they are in sentiment strongly anti-slavery, having great faith in those who are willing to labor with their own hands.

Of this strong anti-slavery sentiment I offer convincing proof in the votes by which they supported in Congress our late highly distinguished representative, Thaddeus Stevens.[*]

---

[*] Traditionary stories exist in our county concerning the Swiss origin, etc., of certain families. I have heard one concerning the Engles, and one of the Stauffers. One of the Johns family has told me of their Swiss origin, and of their name being formerly written Tschantz.

It is probable that other traditionary stories concerning Swiss families could now be collected, if some one would exert himself to do it before their custodians "fall asleep."

But let those who gather these stories beware of the "fine writer," lest he add what he considers embellishments, and make the narratives improbable.

The Stauffer traditions were mentioned to me by a venerable member of the family, one who has kindly lent me his aid and sympathy in some of my records of the "Pennsylvania Dutch."

John Stauffer is now a great-grandfather, and he calculates that it was, at the nearest, his own great-great-grandfather who, with his mother and his three brothers, came to this country, his ancestors being of Swiss origin. " The mother," says my neighbor (in substance), " weighed three hundred, and the sons made a wagon, all of wood, and drawed her to the Rhine. When they got to Philadelphia, they put their mother into the wagon and drawed her up here to Warwick township. There they settled on a pretty spring ; that is what our people like."

The reader of this little story may remember the "pious Æneas," who "from the flames of Troy, upon his shoulders," the old Anchises bore.

The tradition of the Engle family was narrated to me by two of its members.

Mr. Henry M. Engle has felt some difficulty in reconciling the tradition with the fact of the family's having been in this country only about one hundred years, and with his idea that the Swiss persecution must have ceased before that period.

But we have seen that some Baptist families tarried in the Palatinate, etc. before coming here, and a circumstance like the imprisonment of one of their women would be remembered among them for a long time.

Tradition says that it was the grandmother's mother or grandmother of Henry M. Engle and Jacob M. Engle who was a prisoner in Switzerland for her faith. The turnkey's wife is said to have sympathized with the prisoner, because she knew that Annie had children at home. So she said to her, in the Swiss dialect, "Annie, if I were you, I would go away once." (" Annie, wann i die wär, i det mohl geh."—" Annie, wenn ich dich wäre, ich thut einmal gehen.")

She therefore set Annie to washing clothes, and, turning her back upon her, gave her opportunity to escape.

Annie's husband was not a Baptist; nevertheless, he was so friendly as to prepare a hiding-place for her, into which she could go down, if the persecutors came, by means of a trap-door; and she was never taken prisoner again.

THE DUNKER LOVE-FEAST.

On the morning of the 25th of September, 1871, I took the cars of the Pennsylvania Central Railroad for the borough of Mount Joy, in the northwest part of this county. Finding no public conveyance thence to the village of C., I obtained from my landlord a horse and buggy and an obliging driver, who took me four or five miles, for two dollars. We took a drive round by the new Dunker meeting-house, which is a neat frame building,—brown, picked out with white window-frames. Behind it is a wood, upon which the church-doors open, instead of upon the highway.

We heard here that the meeting would not begin till one o'clock on the next day. Some of the brethren were at the church, however, with their teams, having brought provisions, straw, and bedding. We went into the neat meeting-room, and above into the garret, where straw was being laid down. A partition ran down the middle, and upon the women's side a small room

10*   (109)

had also been divided from the rest, wherein were one or two bedsteads and the inevitable cradle. The basement had a hard earthen floor, and was divided into dining-room, kitchen, and cellar. Upon spacious shelves in the cellar a brother and sister were placing the food. Many large loaves of bread were there. The sister was taking pies from a great basket, and bright coffee-pots stood upon the kitchen-table.

All here seemed to speak "Dutch," but several talked English with me. They seemed surprised that I had come so far as twenty-three miles in order to attend the meeting. One remarked that it was no member that had put the notice of the meeting in the paper which I had seen. Others, however, seemed interested, although by my dress it was very plain that I was quite an outsider. I found C. a neat place of about a dozen houses, and we drove to the only tavern. The landlady was young and pleasant, but she could speak little English. She was quite sociable, however, and thought that she could teach me *Dutch* and I her English. By means of some German on my part, we got along tolerably together. She took me to a good chamber, and began removing from it some of their best clothing. Showing me two sun-bonnets, one of them made of black silk, she said, "It is the fashion." "The fashion?" said I. "Yes; the fashion for married women." This was, doubtless, the Dunker influence even among those not members.

Being at leisure in the afternoon, I walked to an ancient Moravian church in the neighborhood, with the landlady's little daughter,—a pretty child.

' Her mother said, " Geh mit der aunty :" so she went with her adopted relative.

" Do you speak English ?" I said to the little one.

" Na!" she answered.

" Hast du ein Bruder ?" (Have you a brother ?) I continued.

" Na!" she replied, in the dialect.

" Wie alt bist du ?" (How old are you ?) I said afterward.*

" Vaze es net." (I don't know.)

Conversation flagged.

I found the church a small log building that had been covered with boards. Many of the tombstones were in the Moravian fashion, such as I had seen at Litiz,—small square slabs, lying flat in the grass; and some were numbered at the top of the inscription. One of these is said to be one hundred and twenty years old, and when it was laid this was doubtless an Indian mission. But the Herrnhüter (as my landlady said) are all

---

* Our " Dutch"—all of them, I believe—use the singular pronoun du, *thou.*

gone, and another society holds meetings in the lowly church.

Although my little guide of six years could not speak English, she was not wanting in good sense. As I was trying to secure the graveyard gate, holding it with one hand, and stooping to roll up the stone that served to keep it fast, the little one, too, put out her hand, unbidden, to hold the gate. I thought that there were some English children that would not have been so helpful, and reflected, as I walked along, upon *unspoken language,* if I may use the expression.

The landlady had a plentiful supper after we returned. I was the only guest, and, as is usual here, the maid sat down with us. We had fried beef, sweet potatoes, pie, very nice apple-butter, canned peaches, barley-coffee, brown sugar, etc. The charge for board was at the rate of one dollar per day.

In the evening I heard my hostess up-stairs preparing my bed, as I supposed. My surprise was therefore considerable, on turning down the woolen coverlet, to find no sheets upon the feather bed. On lifting this light and downy bed, which was neatly covered with white, I found one sheet, a straw bed, and then a bedcord in the place of a sacking-bottom. I at once perceived that the feather bed was a feather cover, of which I had often heard, but had never met with one before during my sojourn in

Pennsylvania "Dutchland." I should think that this downy covering might be pleasant in cold weather, but now I rolled it off upon the floor, and, with the help of a spare comfortable, was soon at rest. The pillow-cases, which were trimmed with edging, were marked with black silk, in a large running-hand, in this manner: "Henry G. Kreider, 1864."

As I sat the next morning awhile with the landlady in her basement kitchen, she remarked, "Here is it as Dutch as Dutchlant." But she said that my Dutch was not like theirs. The neighborhood, however, is not nearly so German as Germany. I was told by an intelligent young man that half the grown men did not speak English: I understand by this, not that they do not speak our language at all, but not habitually and with fluency. Many speak English very well, but the "*Dutch*" accent is universal. For several years the school-books in the township have all been English. I laughed with the landlady, who herself seemed somewhat amused, at the children having English books and speaking Dutch, or, as she would say, " Die Kinner lerne Englisch und schwetze Deitsch." However, at the Dunker church, a pretty girl told me afterward that she had had no difficulty at school the preceding winter, although " we always talk German at home."

At breakfast this morning, among other dishes,

we had raisin-pie. Not a great while after this meal was over, the morning having proved wet, a neighbor took me over to the church in his buggy for twenty-five cents. Although the hour was so early, and meeting was fixed to begin at one, I found a considerable number here, which did not surprise me, as I knew the early habits of our "Dutch" people. Taking a seat, I began to read a number of the *Living Age*, when a black-eyed maid before me, in Dunker dress, handed me her neatly-bound hymn-book, in English and German. I told her that I could read German, and when I read a verse in that language, she said, "But you don't know what it means." Reading German is with us a much rarer accomplishment than speaking the dialect.

Ere long, a stranger came and sat down behind me, and entered into conversation. He was a preacher from a distance, named L., and spoke very good English. We soon found that we had mutual acquaintances in another county, and when dinner was ready he invited me down to partake.

Here the men sat upon one side, and the women on the other, of one of the long tables, upon which was laid a strip of white muslin. We had bowls without spoons, into which was poured by attendant brethren very hot coffee, containing milk or cream, but no sugar. We had the fine Lancaster County bread, good and abundant butter, apple-butter, pickles, and pies. The provisions for these meals are contributed by the members at a previous meeting, where each tells what he intends to furnish, how many loaves of bread, etc., while some prefer to give money.* Whatever food is left over after the four meals are done is given to the poor, without distinction of sect; " whoever needs it most," as a sister said.

At this dinner, before eating, my new acquaintance, L., gave out, by two lines at a time, the verse,

" Eternal are thy mercies, Lord."

But few joined in the singing. They would doubtless have preferred German. In that language thanks were returned after eating.

When we went up into the meeting-room again, a young man of an interesting countenance, a preacher, named Z., asked me if I was not the one who had written an article which had lately appeared in one of our county papers. It was very gratifying to be thus recognized among strangers.

An elderly sister, who sat down by me and began to talk, was named Murphy. The name surprised me much, but it was not the only Irish one here. It is probable that these persons were

---

* To furnish provisions would be natural to a people of whom about seventy-five in a hundred are farmers, as among the Dunkers.

taken into Dunker families when young to be brought up, and thus had been led to join a church so different from the Roman Catholic.

Having observed that there was a good deal of labor to be performed here in waiting upon so many people, I asked Mrs. Murphy whether there were women hired. She told me, "There's a couple of women that's hired; but the members does a heap, too."

On another occasion, I made a remark to a friendly sister about the brethren's waiting upon the table, as they did. She answered that it was according to the Testament to help each other; the women cooked, and the men waited upon the table. She did not seem able to give the text. It may be, "Bear ye one another's burdens." I was amused that it should be so kindly applied to the brethren's helping the sisters.

Before meeting began in the afternoon, a lovely aged brother, with silvery hair and beard, and wearing a woolen coat nearly white, showed me how the seats were made, so that by turning down the backs of some, tables could be formed for the Love-Feast. He told me that the Dunkers number about one hundred thousand,—that they have increased much in the West, but not in the Eastern States. To which I rejoined, smiling, "You Dutch folks do not like poor land, like much of that at the East."

"This is not good land," he said. " We have

improved it;" for I had left the rich limestone soil and had come to the gravelly land in the northern part of the county. But as regards Massachusetts, can it be that there is yet a trace of the ancient antagonism of the Puritans to the Baptists?

When meeting began, as brethren came in, I saw some of these bearded men kissing each other. These holy kisses, as will be seen hereafter, are frequent among the Dunkers, and, as the men shave only the upper lip, it seems strange to us who are unaccustomed to the sight and the sound. The oft-repeated kissing was to me, perhaps, the least agreeable part of the ceremonial.

The afternoon meeting became very crowded, and, as is usual among our "Dutch" people, a number of babies were in attendance. During the sessions their voices sometimes rose high, but the noise did not seem to affect those who were preaching or praying. They felt it perhaps like the wailing and sighing of the wind, which they regard not, and would rather bear the inconvenience of the children than to have the mothers stay away from meeting. This afternoon, during prayer, a little fellow behind me kept saying, " Want to go to pappy;" but if his father was among the brethren, he was on the other side of the house.

My new acquaintance, L., was the only preacher

11

here who spoke in English. All the other exercises, except a little singing, were in German or in our Pennsylvania dialect. This afternoon L. said, among many remarks more sectarian, or less broad, "Faith is swallowed up in sight; hope, in possession ; but charity, or love, is eternal. It came from God, for God is love." The allusion here is to Paul's celebrated panegyric on charity; but how much more charming it is in the German version, "Faith, hope, love; but the greatest of these is love. Love suffereth long and is kind, is not puffed up," etc.

About the middle of the afternoon I perceived a speaker giving some directions, and I asked the women near me what he had said. One answered and said something about "Wahl halten für Prediger," by which I perceived that the election for a preacher was now to take place. Both brethren and sisters were to vote; not to select from a certain set of candidates, however; but at random, among the congregation,—or *Family*, as it is sometimes called ("for all ye are brethren").

In the room above-stairs were the bishop or elder and an assistant to receive the votes. This bishop we might call the father of this family, which has four preachers and as many meeting-houses. The bishop is always that preacher who is oldest in the ministry. Meeting is held by turns in the different houses, occurring only once

in six weeks in the large new house which we
then occupied. These particulars, which I gathered in conversation, are, I believe, substantially
correct.

During the interval of the election I sat and
read, or looked out from my window at the young
people, the gayly-dressed girls mostly grouped
together. Some of these were, probably, relatives of the members, while others may have come
for the ride and the fun, to see and to be seen,—
meetings of this kind being great occasions in the
country-side.

The young men stood around on the outside of
these groups of girls, some holding their whips
and twirling them with the butts resting upon
the ground. Of course the young girls were not
conscious of the presence of the beaux.

On the front of the house, or rather the back,
—for, as I have said, the main doors open upon
the wood instead of upon the roadside,—were
more young girls, and plain sisters and brethren.

I asked a nice-looking woman about the election, but she could not tell me, although she
wore the plain cap. "Most of the women do
around here," she said, and added that Dunker
women in meeting had offered to kiss her.
"You know they greet each other with a kiss."

After the brethren, the sisters were called up
to vote. I laughed, in talking with some of
the members, at the women's being allowed to

vote, in contrast to the usual custom.   Mrs. Murphy reckoned it would be different if the women should undertake to vote for Governor or President.

I said to some of the sisters, "Who do you think will be chosen?"   But they pleasantly informed me that to talk upon this point was against their rules,—it was a matter for internal reflection.

After meeting was over next day, as the bishop was talking with a sister, I ventured to ask him whether a majority was necessary to elect a preacher, or only a plurality.   He seemed quite willing to talk, displaying no clerical pride, and answered, "A majority," adding, "Do you speak German?"   I feared that I could not readily understand him on such a subject, and put the case to him thus in English : "Suppose one man has twenty votes, another fifteen, and another ten?" Then the bishop said that the one having twenty would be elected; whence it seems that a plurality only is required.   On this occasion the vote was doubtless much divided, for I afterward heard that the bishop had said to the congregation that it seemed there were a good many there that were thought fit for preachers.

As sunset approached, some of the members began to form tables from the benches, for the Love-Feast, which made me wonder when supper was to be ready.   I soon found, however, that my ignorance of the language had pre-

vented my observing that while the "Family"
voted the rest of the congregation supped. I
was told, however, that if I would go down I
could still get something to eat. These meals
were free to every one that came. All were received, in the hope that they would obtain some
spiritual good.

In the basement I found a number of men
sitting at the end of one of the tables, waiting
for food, and I also sat down near them. I was
invited, however, by a sister to step into the
kitchen, where I stood and partook of hot coffee, bread and butter, etc. As we went along
through the dining-room, I thought that the
sister cast a reproachful glance at a disorderly
man seated at the table with his whip, and who
was, perhaps, intoxicated. I wondered that she
should have taken me from the table to stand
in the kitchen, till I remembered that that was
a men's table.

In the kitchen, brethren were busily occupied
cutting large loaves of bread into quarters for
the coming Love-Feast; and when I returned to
the room above, active preparations were still
going on, which consumed much time. The im-
provised tables were neatly covered with white
cloths, and hanging lamps shed down light upon
the scene. Piles of tin pans were placed upon
the table, knives, forks, and spoons, and sometimes a bowl. The tables occupied nearly the

whole floor of the church, leaving but little
room for spectators. I was myself crowded
into a corner, where the stairs came up from
the basement and went up to the loft; but,
though at times I was much pressed for room,
I had an excellent place to observe, for I stood
at the end of the main table. Here stood, too,
a bright and social sister from a neighboring
congregation, who did not partake of the feast,
and was able and willing to explain the ceremonial to me, in English,—Mrs. R., as I will call
her.

Near by at the table, among the older sisters,
sat a pair who attracted a great deal of my
attention—a young mother and her babe—herself so quiet, and such a quiet babe! They
might have been photographed. Once or twice
the little six-weeks' child gave a feeble young
wail, and I saw the youthful mother modestly
give it that nourishment which nature provides.

The brethren came up carrying tubs of meat,
which smelt savory, for I was fasting from flesh
since the morning. Then came great vessels of
soup,—one of them a very large tin wash-boiler.
The soup was taken out into the tin pans before
mentioned, and the plates of meat were set upon
the top, as if to keep both hot. And, now that
"at the long last" the Love-Feast tables were
spread, the fasting family was ready to begin,
not the supper, but the feet-washing! This was

the more remarkable, because the Testament, their rule of action, relates that, supper being ended, Jesus washed the disciples' feet.

The bishop arose in his place at the table, and, lamp in one hand and book in the other, read in German the account of the feet-washing in John's Gospel.

Four men who stood in front of him, watching his words, started when he said "legte seine Kleider ab" ("laid aside his garments"), and, in imitation of Jesus, took off their coats; and, as the Scripture says, "He took a towel and girded himself," they, or two of them, put on long white aprons, tied around the waist. Two washed feet and two wiped, and then he who was thus ministered unto was kissed by one or both of the ministering brethren. I was a little surprised that two should perform that office, which Jesus is said to have performed alone; but Mrs. R. told me that, as the Church was one body, it was considered that it made no difference to have two persons.

The four who had ministered took their seats, and were served in their turn, four others taking their places, and so on. Upon the sisters' side of the house, on a front bench, the sisters were, in a similar manner, performing the same ordinance.

While the religious services of the evening were going on within, from without there came the sound of voices and laughter,—from where the young people *of the world* were enjoying themselves in the clear, cool moonlight. I doubt not that, by this time, the girls had recognized the presence of the young men.

Once there was a shriek or a yell, and Mrs. R. said, "Oh, the drunken rowdies! there's always some of them here!"

Having heard of the non-resistant or *wehrlos* tenets of the Dunkers, I wondered what they would do should the disturbance without become very great and unpleasant. Mrs. Murphy thought that the other people would interfere in such a case,—that is, that those not members would interest themselves to maintain order. But on this point I afterward received information from a brother, as I shall mention. The services were so long that I told Mrs. R. I thought that the soup would be cold. "Oh, no!" she said, "that won't get cold so soon." So I ventured to put my finger against a pan near me, and it was yet warm. She asked me, during feet-washing, whether I did not think that I would feel happy to be there, partaking of that exercise.

I answered, in a non-committal manner, that if I had been brought up to such things, as she had been, I might feel so, but that all my friends and acquaintances were of a different mind. She rejoined, "But we must follow Christ, and serve

God, in spite of the world." Even after the feet
were all washed, the fasting family could not yet
eat, on account of the protracted exhortations.

At length they broke their fast. From two
to four persons, each with a spoon, ate together
from one pan of soup, very quietly, fifty feed-
ing like one, so to speak, the absence of sound
proceeding in part from the absence of earthen
plates. Then they cut from the meat and from
the quarter-loaves, and partook of the butter,
these being all the food. There was no salt nor
any other condiment. The occasional bowl was
for water. I suppose that most persons would
think that there had been enough kissing of the
kind; but about this time a young bishop, an
assistant, stood up at the centre of the main
table, and after some remarks shook hands
with the sister upon his left and kissed the
brother upon his right, and from brother to
brother, and from sister to sister, the kiss went
around the congregation.

The bishop, and this assistant, went around
upon ours, the women's side, superintending
this ceremony, as if to see that none failed in
this expression of unity, and that it was conducted in an orderly manner. The last sister
who has no one to kiss goes forward, and
kisses the first one, with whom the bishop had
shaken hands, thus completing the chain of
unity. This was doubtless done before the

Communion, and showed that brotherly love existed among these brethren, fitting them to partake of the Sacrament. I was also told that the latter half of the afternoon meeting had been for self-examination on the same subject.

About this time of the evening Mrs. R. told me that if I would go down I could get some of the soup, as there was plenty left. I was willing to partake, not having had a regular supper, and I got a bowl of good mutton-broth, containing rice or barley, etc.

After the Love-Feast, these " Old Brethren," as they are· sometimes called, held the Communion. The bread and wine were placed upon the general or main table—being set before the bishops—and were covered with a white cloth.

Before the celebration of the ordinance, there was read in German the passage of Scripture upon which it is founded; and also, as it seemed to me, the narrative of the crucifixion. The hymn now sung was an English one, and the only one in our language that was sung by the whole congregation during the two days' meeting. It was,

"Alas ! and did my Saviour bleed."

Meantime, the assistant bishop divided the bread, or cakes, which were unleavened and sweetened. He directed the members, while eating the bread, to reflect upon the sufferings of the Saviour. His manner was devout and impressive. As he and Bishop D—— passed around among the women, distributing the bread, the former repeated several times, in a sonorous voice, these or similar words: "Das Brod das wir brechen ist die Gemeinschaft des Leibes Christi." ("The bread that we break is the communion of the body of Christ.")

The wine, which smelt strong, was the juice of the grape, and was made in the neighborhood. An aged bishop from another congregation made some observations, and while speaking marked the length of something upon his finger. Mrs. R. said that he was showing the size of the thorns in the crown. She added, "They are there yet." I looked at her in much surprise, wondering whether she believed in the preservation of the actual thorns; whereupon she added, "They grow there still. Did you never read it in Bausman's book on the Holy Land?— Bausman, the Reformed preacher." The simplicity of the surroundings upon this occasion were, it seemed to me, in keeping with those of the original Supper, at which sat the "Carpenter's Son" and the fishermen.

When meeting was over, as I did not see my escort to the public house, and as I had been told that I could stay here, I followed those who went above-stairs, and received a bolster made of a grain-bag filled with hay or straw. I shared it with Mrs. Murphy. Our bed was composed of straw laid upon the floor, and covered, or nearly so, with pieces of domestic carpet. We had a coverlet to lay over us. I talked with some of the other women who lay beside us, and could not get to sleep immediately; but at last I slept so sweetly that it was not agreeable to be disturbed at four o'clock, when the sisters, by my reckoning, began to rise. When some of these had gone down, I should perhaps have slept again, had it not been for a continued talking upon the men's side of the partition, quite audible, as the partition only ran up to a distance of some feet, not nearly so high as the lofty ridge of the building. The voices appeared to be those of a young man and one or two boys, talking in the dialect. A woman near me laughed.

"What is it?" said I.

"It's too mean to tell," she answered.

I surmise that the Dunker brethren had gone down and left these youths. Although a baby was crying, I lay still until two girls in Dunker caps—one ten years old, the other twelve—came with a candle, looking at us, smiling, and making remarks, perhaps thinking that it was time for us to be up.

I asked the eldest what o'clock it was.

She did not know.

"What made you get up, then?"

"I got up when the others did."

Then some one explained that there were a good many dishes left unwashed the evening before.

I was surprised to see such young persons members of the meeting, for I supposed that the Dunkers, like the Mennonites, are opposed to infant baptism. The former explained to me, however, that they thought such persons as these old enough to distinguish right from wrong. I was told, too, of one girl, still younger, who had insisted on *wearing the cap.* The Mennonites baptize persons as young as fifteen. Both sects seem to hold peculiar views upon original sin.

A Dunker preacher once said to me,—

"We believe that, after Adam, all were born in sin; but, after Christ, all were born without sin."

And a Mennist neighbor says,—

"Children have no sin; the kingdom of heaven is of little children."

I continued to lie still, looking at the rafters and roof, and speculating as to their being so clean, and clear of cobwebs, and whether they had been laboriously swept; and then, gathering my wardrobe together with some little trouble, I was at last ready to go down. As I went to one of the windows, I saw Orion and Sirius, and the coming day.

Going down to wash at the pump, in the morning gloaming, while the landscape still lay in shade, I found two or three lads at the pump, and one of them pumped for me. I was so ignorant of pump-washing as to wonder why he pumped so small a stream, and to suspect that he was *making fun;* but thus it seems it is proper to do, to avoid wetting the sleeves.

Here I met a pretty young sister, from Cumberland County,—fat and fair,—whose acquaintance I had made the day before. Her cap was of lace, and not so plain as the rest. There was with her at the pump one of the world's people, a young girl in a blue dress.

"Is that your sister?" I asked.

"It's the daughter of the woman I live with," she replied. "I have no sister. I am hired with her mother."

To my inexperienced eye it was not easy to tell the rich Dunkers from the poor, when all wore so plain a dress. I was afterward much surprised on discovering that this pretty sister did not understand German. Another from Cumberland County told me that I ought to come to their meeting, which was nearly all English.

After washing I went up into the meeting-house, where the lamps were yet burning. A few sisters were sitting here, and two little maidens were making a baby laugh and scream by walking her back and forth along the empty benches. About sunrise the bishop had arrived, and a number of brethren ranged themselves upon the benches and began to sing. Before long, we, who had stayed over-night, had our breakfast, having cold meat at this and the succeeding meal. I think it was at breakfast that my pleasant friend with the silvery hair mentioned that there was still a store of bread and pies.

The great event of the morning meeting was the "making the preacher." At my usual seat, at a distant window, I was so busily occupied with my notes that I did not perceive what was going on at the preacher's table, until I saw a man and woman standing before the table with their backs to the rest of the congregation. I made my way to my former corner of observation, and found that there was another brother standing with them, the sister in the middle, and these were receiving the greetings of the Family. The brethren came up, one by one, kissed one of the men, shook hands with the sister, and kissed the other man. This last was the newly-chosen preacher, the former brother, named Z., being a preacher who, by the consent of the members (also given yesterday), was now advanced one degree in the ministry, and was henceforth to have power to marry and to baptize. The sister was his wife. She is expected to support her husband in the ministry, and to be ready to receive those women who, after baptism, come up from the water. This office and that of voting seem to be the only important ones held by women in this society. Herein they differ greatly from another plain sect,— Friends or Quakers, among whom women minister, transact business, etc.*

After the brethren were done, the sisters came

---

* A friend tells me that he once heard a discourse from a celebrated Dunker preacher, named Sarah Reiter. She was allowed to preach, it seems, by a liberal construction of Paul's celebrated edict, because she was unmarried.

Even when afterward married, by a more liberal construction still, the liberty to preach was not forbidden her. Possibly it was assumed that her *husband at home* was not able to answer all her questions upon spiritual matters. She removed to Ohio.

In the Encyclopædia Americana, the following are given as propositions of some of the former Anabaptists : "Impiety prevails everywhere. It is therefore necessary that a new family of holy persons should be founded, enjoying without distinction of sex the gift of prophecy, and skill to interpret divine revelations. Hence they need no learning, for the internal word is more than the outward expression."

At this time, however, while our German Baptists still believe in an unpaid, untaught ministry, none of them, I think, hold to the doctrine that the gift of prophecy or preaching is without distinction of sex.

In this respect, George Fox seems to have agreed with the early Anabaptists just mentioned.

up, shook hands with Z., kissed his wife, and shook hands with the new preacher, whose wife, I believe, was not present.

The bishop invited the sisters to come forward: "Koomet alle! alle die will. Koomet alle!"

While this salutation was in progress, L., who spoke in English, made some explanatory remarks. He told us that he had read or heard of two men traveling together, of whom one was a doctor of divinity. The latter asked the younger man what he was now doing. He replied that he was studying divinity. He had formerly been studying law, but on looking around he saw no opening in the law, so he was now studying divinity, which course or which change met the approval of the reverend doctor.

"Now," said L., "*we* do not approve of men-made preachers;" a striking remark in a congregation where a preacher had just been elected by a plurality. But he went on to explain that he trusted that there was no brother or sister who had voted for him who had just been chosen for this arm of the church, who had not prayed God earnestly that they might make such a choice as would be profitable in the church. He went on to explain that the newly-chosen preacher was now receiving from the congregation an expression of unity.

There were various other exercises this morning,—preaching, praying, and singing,—before the final adjournment. At the close we had dinner. I made an estimate of the number who partook of this meal as about five hundred and fifty. One of the men guessed a thousand; but we are prone to exaggerate numbers where our feelings are interested.

Before we parted, I had some conversation with certain brethren, principally upon the non-resistant doctrines of the society. In my own neighborhood, not a great while before, a Dunker had been robbed under peculiar circumstances. Several men had entered his house at night, and, binding him and other members of the family, had forced him to tell where his United States and other bonds were placed, and had carried off property worth four thousand dollars. The brother had gone in pursuit of them, visiting the mayor of our town, and the police in neighboring cities (without recovering his property). I asked these brethren at different times whether his course was in agreement with their rules. They answered that it was not.

On the present occasion I repeated the question as to what they would have done on the previous evening if the disturbance had risen to a great height. One of the brethren, in reply, quoted from the Acts of the Apostles, where it is narrated that forty Jews entered into a conspiracy to kill Paul. But Paul sent his nephew to the chief captain to inform him of the conspiracy.

The captain then put Paul under the charge of soldiers, to be brought safe unto Felix the governor.

From this passage the Dunkers feel at liberty to appeal to the police for their protection, but only once; if protection be not then afforded them, they must do without it.

I further mentioned to these brethren a case which had been told to me some time before by a Dunker preacher, of a certain brother who had been sued in the settlement of an estate, and had received a writ from the sheriff. This writ was considered by the Dunkers as a call from the powers that be, to whom they are ordered to be subservient, and the brother therefore went with some brethren to the office of a lawyer, who furnished him with subpœnas to summon witnesses in his defence. But the Dunkers argued among themselves that for him to take these legal papers from his pocket would be to draw the sword. He therefore sent word to his friends, informally, to come to the office of a magistrate; and, the evidence being in his favor, he was released. "This," said my informant, "is the only lawsuit that I have known in our society since I joined the meeting," which was, I believe, a period of about seven years.

In repeating this narrative to the brethren at the Love-Feast, I learned that they are now at liberty to engage in defensive lawsuits. They have, as I understood one to say, no creed and no discipline (although I believe that a certain confession of faith is required). The New Testament (or, as they say, the Testament) they claim to be their creed and their discipline. There is also much independence in the congregations. But in some cases they have resort to a general council, and here it has been decided that a Dunker may defend himself in a lawsuit, but only once. Should an appeal be taken to another court, the Dunker can go no farther. This reminds me of Paul's question to the Corinthians, " Why do you not rather suffer loss than go to law?"* Does it not seem hard to practice such non-resistance, to remain upright and open-minded, and at the same time to acquire much wealth?

The Dunkers do not like to be called by this name. Their chosen title is Brethren.

The Love-Feast, above described, was held by the " Old Brethren," who originated in Germany about the year 1708.

It has been said that they originated among the Pietists; but a very great resemblance will be found among them to our German Baptists of the Mennonite or Anabaptist stock.

I afterward visited other Dunkers, belonging to a division called the " River Brethren." They originated

---

* See the questions in full,—I. Corinthians, chap. vi.

near the Susquehanna River, but they have now spread as far as Ohio, if not farther.

That these are of the old Baptist stock there is no doubt, as Jacob Engle, their founder, was of a Mennonite family,—a family which boasts that one of their ancestors was a prisoner in Switzerland on account of her faith. (See note on " Swiss Exiles.")

In coming to this country, about one hundred years ago, tradition tells us that the Engle family joined with thirty others, who were upon the same vessel, to remain bound together in life and in death. The young infants of these families all died upon the voyage, except Jacob Engle, whereupon an old nurse said, " God has preserved him for an especial purpose."

He became a preacher, and this his friends regarded as a fulfillment of the prophecy.

Jacob Engle, or " Yokely Engle," as he was sometimes called, considered that there was not sufficient warmth and zeal among the Mennonites at that time.

He became very zealous; experiencing, as he believed, a change of heart.

Before he became a preacher, some joined him in holding prayer-meetings. It was found that some wished to be baptized by immersion, and the rite was thus performed (whereas the Mennonites baptize by pouring).

A common observer would see very little difference between these Brethren and the Old Dunkers. The River Brethren allow all present to partake of the Love-Feast, or Paschal Supper. Some of them have said that the Paschal Supper is an expression of the love of God to all mankind, and love toward all men constrains them to invite all to partake thereof. But from the Lord's Supper they exclude all strangers.

Their meetings are usually held in private houses, or, in summer, in barns.

Some of their preachers have been heard, upon rising to speak, to declare that they intend to say only what the Spirit teaches them.

One of their most striking peculiarities is their opposition to the use of lightning-rods. A preacher said to me, when talking upon this subject, " If God wishes to preserve the building, he can preserve it without the lightning-rod. If he does not wish to preserve it, I am willing to submit to the result."

It has been thought that an acquaintance with the laws of electricity would remove this objection which they feel.

The Brinser Brethren were formed from the River Brethren some years ago. They are popularly thus called from an able preacher named Matthias Brinser. They erect meeting-houses, in preference, as I understand, to meeting in private houses. Their church has not opposed electrical conductors, though some members feel conscientious in the matter.

The question of erecting meeting-houses seems to have caused considerable trouble among the River Brethren. A gentleman of our county remarked to me that the custom of meeting in private houses is traditional among our people, and dates from times of persecution.

EPHRATA.

Tнιs quiet village in Lancaster County has been for over a century distinguished as the seat of a Protestant monastic institution, established by the Seventh-Day German Baptists about the year 1738.

Conrad Beissel, the founder of the cloister, was born in Germany, at Oberbach, in the Palatinate, in the year 1691.

He was by trade a baker, but, after coming to this country, he worked at weaving with Peter Becker, the Dunker preacher, at Germantown.

He is said to have been a Presbyterian, which I interpret a member of the German Reformed Church.

According to the inscription upon his tombstone, his "spiritual life" began in 1716, or eight years before he was baptized among the Dunkers.

This may be explained by an article written by the Rev. Christian Endress,* who seems to

---

* See Hazard's Register, vol. v. C. L. F. Endress, D.D., preached twelve years in Trinity (Lutheran) Church, Lancaster.

(139)

have studied the Ephrata Community more, in connection with their published writings,* than have the mass of persons who have endeavored to describe this peculiar people.*

Mr. Endress says, "The Tunkers trace their origin from the Pietists near Schwarzenau, in Germany.†

While they yet belonged among the Pietists, there was a society formed at Schwarzenau composed of eight persons, whose spiritual leader was Alexander Mack, a miller of Schriesheim.

The members of this little society are said to have been re-baptized (by immersion), because they considered their infant baptism as unavail-

---

* At the present time, the learned Dr. Seidensticker, of Philadelphia, is preparing an article upon this subject. To him, and to Mr. J. D. Rupp, I am indebted for assistance.

† A new movement in German theology arose in the second half of the seventeenth century, through Spener, the founder of Pietism. The central principle of Pietism was that Christianity was first of all life, and that the strongest proof of the truth of its doctrines was to be found in the religious experience of the believing subject. The principles of the Pietists were in the main shared by the Moravians. (See American Cyclopædia, article *German Theology.*) Compare this statement of the main principle of Pietism with this of the Anabaptists, whom the mass of our Dunkers so much resemble: "The opinions common to the Anabaptists are founded on the principle that Christ's kingdom on earth, or the church, is a visible society of pious and holy persons, with none of those institutions which human sagacity has devised for the ungodly." (See American Cyclopædia, article *Anabaptist.*)

ing, and to have first assumed the name of Taeuffer, or Baptists.*

The Dunkers first appeared in America in 1719, when about twenty families landed in Philadelphia, and dispersed to Germantown, Conestoga, and elsewhere.

Beissel was baptized among them in 1724, in Pequea Creek, a tributary of the Susquehanna. He lived for awhile at Mühlbach (or Mill Creek, —now in Lebanon County ?). About a year after his baptism, he published a tract upon the Seventh Day as the true Sabbath. This tract caused a disturbance among the brethren at Mill Creek, and about three years after, in 1728, Beissel and some with him withdrew from the other Dunkers, and Beissel re-baptized those of his own society.

Not long after, says Endress, Beissel, who had appointed several elders over his people, withdrew from them, and retired to live a solitary life in a cottage that had been built for a similar purpose, and occupied by a brother called Elimelech. This cottage stood near the place where the convent was afterward built.

Here we infer that he lived for several years.

---

* They took for themselves the name of Brethren, says an article in Rupp's "Religious Denominations." The Dunkers in our county call themselves Brethren,—"Old Brethren," "River Brethren," etc. Whether the Ephrata Dunkers adopted the same name, I cannot say.

To live the life of cenobites or hermits, says Rupp, was in some measure peculiar to many of the Pietists who had fled from Germany to seek an asylum in Pennsylvania. "On the banks of the Wissahickon, near Philadelphia, severil hermits had their cells, some of them men of fine talents and profound erudition."

Of some of these hermits, and of the monastic community afterward settled at Ephrata, it is probable that a ruling idea was the speedy coming of Christ to judge the world.

It is stated that after the formation of Beissel's "camp" (or *Lager*) midnight meetings were held, for some time, to await the coming of judgment.

Those who remember the Millerite, or Second Advent, excitement of the year 1843, can appreciate the effect that this idea would have upon the minds of the Dunkers, and how it could stimulate them to suffer many inconveniences for the brief season that they expected to tarry in the world.*

While Beissel was dwelling in his solitary cot, about the year 1730, two married women joined the society, of whom the Ephrata Chronicle tells us that they left their husbands and placed them-

---

* In the time of the Millerite excitement above alluded to, many prepared ascension robes. One person whom I heard of went to the roof of his house, where, in his robe, he could look for the coming of Christ, and where he was prepared immediately to ascend.

selves under the lead of the director (or Vorsteher, the title applied to Beissel in the " Chronicon"). He received them, although it was against the canon of the new society. One of these was Maria Christiana, the wife of Christopher Sower, he who afterward established the celebrated German printing-office at Germantown. She escaped in the year 1730, and was baptized the same fall. In the beginning, she dwelt alone in the desert, "and showed by her example that a manly spirit can dwell in a female creature."*

While Beissel was still in his hermitage, discord and strife arose among the brethren of his society, news of which reached him by some means, for in the year 1733 he cited them to appear at his cottage.

They met, and some of the single brethren agreed to build a second cottage near that occupied by their leader. Besides this, a house was also built for females, and in May, 1733, two single women retired into it.†

In 1734, a third house for male brethren was

---

* " Afterward, she held to edification for many years, in the Sister-convent, the office of a sub-prioress, under the name of Marcella. Finally, in her age, she was induced by her son to return to her husband—although another motive was the severe manner of life in the Encampment, which she could no longer bear."—*Chronicon Ephratense*, p. 45.

† Are these the married women just spoken of, who had become single?

built and occupied by the brothers Onesimus and Jotham, whose family name was Eckerlin.*

---

* These remarkable men seem to deserve especial notice.

In Rupp's History of Lancaster County, it is stated that they were from Germany, and had been brought up Catholics. Israel Eckerlin (Brother Onesimus) became prior of the Brother-House at Ephrata. Peter Miller, in an original letter, complains that he obliged them to meddle with worldly things further than their obligations permitted; and that when money came in it was put out at interest, "contrary to our principles."

They could not, however, have been very rich, for when in 1745 a bell arrived in Philadelphia, from England, which had been ordered by Eckerlin, and which cost eighty pounds, they knew not how to pay for it. The name of Onesimus had been placed upon the bell.

When the news of its arrival was received, a council was held in the presence of the spiritual father, Beissel, and it was concluded to break the bell to pieces and bury it in the earth.

The next morning, however, the father appeared in the council, and said that he had reflected that as the Brothers were poor, the bell should be pardoned. It therefore was sold, and was placed upon the Lutheran church in Lancaster.

Miller says that the prior (Eckerlin) conceived a notion to make himself independent of Beissel, and was stripped of all his dignities.

The Eckerlins, says Rupp, afterward moved to Virginia. In Day's Historical Collections, article Greene County, it is stated that three brothers named Eckarly, Dunkards by profession, left the eastern parts of Pennsylvania and plunged into the western wilderness. Their first permanent camp was on a creek flowing into the Monongahela, in Pennsylvania, to which stream they gave the name of Dunkard Creek, which it still bears. These men of peace employed themselves in exploring the country in every direction.

They afterward removed to Dunkards' Bottom, on Cheat

Soon after, says Endress, they all united in the building of a bake-house and a storehouse for the poor. And now the whole was called the camp (*das Lager*).

About this time, he continues, there was what the Tunkers called a revival in Falconer Swamp,

River, which they made their permanent residence; "and, with a savage war raging at no considerable distance, they spent some years unmolested."

In the same narrative it is stated that Dr. Thomas Eckarly, in order to obtain salt, ammunition, and clothing, recrossed the mountains with some skins. Upon his return, he was unavoidably detained. On approaching the cabin where he had left his brothers, he found a heap of ashes. "In the yard lay the mangled and putrid remains of the two brothers," and the hoops on which their scalps had been dried.

This seems a very sorrowful termination to the lives of men of peace, but the reader may be consoled by hearing Miller's account of the brothers,—who are but two, it appears in his narrative.

He says, "The prior quitted the camp, and established a new settlement for hermits on the banks of the new river." (Ohio?)

After many vicissitudes, he and his brother were taken prisoners by seven Mohawks, and sold to Quebec, whence they were transported to France, "where, after our prior had received the tonsure and become a friar of their church, they both died." The Ephrata Chronicle says (chap. xxiii.) that the prior went *out of time* twenty years before Beissel. The latter died in 1768. By the former reckoning, the prior went out of time in 1748, or about three years after the difficulty about the bell at Ephrata. It is possible that his death is antedated in the Chronicle; but history, like other human evidence, is sometimes a strange thing.

(Day, after speaking of the Eckerlins at Ephrata, refers us to the Greene County narrative, above given in brief.)

13*

in consequence of which many families took up land round about the camp, and moved upon it. Another revival on the banks of the Schuylkill drove many more into the neighborhood; by it the Sister establishment gained accessions; but only two, Drusilla and Basilla, remained steadfast. "A further revival in Tolpehoccon," 1735, brought many to the society. Hereupon they built a meeting-house, with rooms attached to it for the purpose of holding [preparing?] love-feasts, and called it Kedar. About the same time, a revival in Germantown sent additional Brothers and Sisters to the camp.

It was in 1735, during the revival at Tulpe-hocken, that Peter Miller was baptized.* Miller, in one of his letters (see Hazard's Register, vol. xvi.), speaks of several persons who, as it appears, were baptized with him; namely, the school-master, three *Elderlings* (one of them Conrad Weyser), five families, and some single persons. This, he says, raised such a fermentation in that church (by which I suppose he means the Re-formed Church, which they left), that a persecution might have followed had the magistrates consented with the generality.

---

* The Tulpehocken Creek is a tributary of the Schuylkill, which rises in Lebanon County, and empties at Reading, in Berks County. It was, I suppose, within the limits of Lebanon County, with perhaps adjoining parts of Berks, that Miller preached.

Peter Miller, whom we are now quoting, was one of the most remarkable men that joined the Ephrata Baptists. He was born in the Palatinate, and is said to have been educated at Heidelberg. He came to this country when about twenty years old. He is mentioned, it seems, in an interesting letter of the Rev. Jedediah Andrews, under date of Philadelphia, 1730, which letter may be found in Hazard's Register. He says that there are "in this province a vast number of Palatines. Those that have come of late years are mostly Presbyterian, or, as they call themselves, Reformed, the Palatines being about three-fifths of that sort of people."

Mr. Andrews says, in substance, "There is lately come over a Palatine candidate for the ministry, who applied to us at the Synod for ordination. He is an extraordinary person for sense and learning. His name is John Peter Miller,* and he speaks Latin as readily as we do our vernacular tongue."†

---

* In Rupp's "Thirty Thousand Names" of immigrants to Pennsylvania, there will be found under date of August 29th, 1730, the names of Palatines with their families, imported in the ship Thistle of Glasgow, from Rotterdam, last from Cowes. Among these occurs Peter Müller, whom by a note Rupp connects with the Peter Miller of the text.

As to the name John Peter, as given by Andrews, it is surprising to see how many of these immigrants bear the names of John, Hans, Johan, Johann, and Johannes, prefixed to other names. I count twenty in a column of thirty-four.

† Mr. Andrews, from whom I quote, was a graduate of

Peter Miller, in one of his letters, speaks of his baptism (or re-baptism) in the year 1735. He says at that time the solitary Brethren and Sisters lived dispersed "in the wilderness of Canestogues, each for himself, as heremits, and I following that same way did set up my hermitage in Dulpchakin [Tulpehocken], at the foot of a mountain, on a limpid spring; the house is still extant [1790], with an old orchard. There did I lay the foundation of solitary life.*

"However," he continues, "I had not lived there half a year, when a great change happened; for a camp was laid out for all solitary persons, at the very spot where now Ephrata stands, and where at that same time the president [Beissel] lived with some heremits. And now, when all heremits were called in, I also quitted my solitude, and changed the same for a monastic life; which was judged to be more inservient to sanctification than the life of a

---

Harvard, who seems to have come to Philadelphia in 1698, and to have preached in an Independent or Presbyterian church, or both.

* The Conestogas were a small tribe . . . consisting in all of some dozen or twenty families, who dwelt a few miles below Lancaster. They sent messengers with corn, venison, and skins, to welcome William Penn. When the whites began to settle around them, Penn assigned them a residence on the manor of Conestoga. (See Day's Historical Collections.) The Conestoga Creek empties into the Susquehanna, below Lancaster.

heremit, where many under a pretence of holiness did nothing but nourish their own selfishness. . . . We were now, by necessity, compelled to learn obedience. . . . At that time, works of charity hath been our chief occupation.*

"Canestogues was then a great wilderness, and began to be settled by poor Germans, which desired our assistance in building houses for them; which not only kept us employed several summers in hard carpenter's-work, but also increased our poverty so much that we wanted even things necessary for life."

He also says, "When we settled here, our number was forty Brethren, and about so many Sisters,† all in the vigor and prime of their ages, never before wearied of social life, but were compelled, . . . with reluctance of our nature, to select this life."‡

---

* When this letter was written, Miller was about eighty years old. He doubtless spoke German during the sixty years that he lived at Ephrata, as well as before that time. It will be observed that he does not write English elegantly.

† In the year 1740, says Fahnestock, there were thirty-six single Brethren in the cloisters, and thirty-five Sisters; and at one time the society, including the members living in the neighborhood, numbered nearly three hundred.

‡ Rev. C. Endress says that some were anxious to retain the solitary life, and some (it appears) were opposed to giving to Beissel the title of Father. Sangmeister left the society and retired to a solitary life in Virginia. "His book," says the

It was, as it appears, about the same time that Miller was baptized .that the midnight meetings were- held at the camp, "for the purpose of awaiting the coming of judgment."

Not long after the building of the meeting-house called Kedar (says Endress), a widower, Sigmund Lambert, having joined the camp, built out of his own means an addition to the meeting-house and a dwelling for Beissel. Another gave all his property to the society, and now Kedar was transformed into a Sister-convent, and a new meeting-house was erected.

Soon after 1738, a large house for the Brethren was built, called Zion, and the whole camp was named Ephrata.*

The solitary life was changed into the conventual one; Zion was called a Kloster, or convent, and put under monastic rules. Onesimus (Eckerlin) was appointed prior, and Conrad Beissel named Father.†

It was probably about this time, or before, that the constable entered the camp, according

---

same writer, "is much tainted with bitterness, and undertakes to cast a dark shade upon the whole establishment."

* Larger accommodations were afterward built in the meadow below; a Sister-house, called Saron, a Brother-house, named Bethania, etc. Most of these are still standing, I believe, in 1872; but the former buildings on the hill long since disappeared.

† His general title appears to be *Vorsteher*, superintendent or principal.

to Miller, and demanded the single man's tax. Some paid, but some refused. Miller says that some claimed personal immunity on the ground that "we were not inferior" to the monks and hermits in the Eastern country, who supplied the prisons in Alexandria with bread, and who were declared free of taxes by Theodosius the Great and other emperors. But these Ephrata Brethren were not to be thus exempted. Six lay in prison at Lancaster ten days, when they were released on bail of a "venerable old justice of peace." When the Brethren appeared before the board of assessment, the gentlemen who were their judges saw six men who in the prime of their ages had been reduced to skeletons by penitential works. The gentlemen granted them their freedom on condition that they should be taxed as one family for their real estate, "which is still in force (1790), although these things happened fifty years ago." (See Miller's letters in Hazard's Register.)

A monastic dress was adopted by the Brethren and Sisters, resembling that of the Capuchins.*

---

* The Ephrata Chronicle speaks nearly in this manner of that of the Sisters:

Their dress was ordered, like that of the Brethren, so that little was to be seen of the disagreeable human figure (von dem verdriesslichen Bild das durch die Sünd ist offenbar worden). They wore caps like the Brethren, but not pointed ones. While at work, these caps or cowls hung down their

The Chronicle, published in 1786, speaks of the Sisters as having carefully maintained the dress of the order for nearly fifty years. About the same date we read of Miller in his cowl.

It appears from the Chronicle that the other members of the society at one time adopted a similar dress, but that the celibates (die Einsamen) appeared at worship in white dresses, and the other members (die Hausstände) in gray ones. The secular members, however, "saddled themselves again" and conformed to the world in clothing and in other things.

In an article upon Ephrata in Hazard's Register, vol. v., 1830, will be found the statement that, thirty or forty years before, the Dunkers were occasionally noticed in Philadelphia (when they came down with produce), with long beards and Capuchin habiliments; but this statement does not seem to agree in date with that of the Chronicle, if these were secular brethren.

Among the austerities practiced at Ephrata

---

backs; but when they saw anybody, they drew them over their heads, so that but little could be seen of their faces. But the principal token of their spiritual betrothal was a great veil, which in front covered them altogether, and behind down to the girdle. Roman Catholics who saw this garment said that it resembled the habit of the scapular.

At Ephrata, in the winter of 1872, Sister ——— showed me in the Sister-house a garment of white cotton, composed of the cowl, to which were attached long pieces before and behind, coming down, I think, nearly to the feet.

formerly, was sleeping upon a bench with a block of wood for a pillow.*

A recent writer, Dr. William Fahnestock, tells us that these and other austerities were not intended for penance, but were undertaken from economy. Their circumstances were very restricted, and their undertaking was great. They studied the strictest simplicity and economy. For the Communion they used wooden flagons, goblets, and trays. The plates from which they ate were thin octagonal pieces of poplar board, their forks and candlesticks were of wood, and every article that could be made of that substance was used by the whole community.

Rupp says that the chimneys, which remain in use to this day (1844), are of wood; and the attention of the present writer in 1872 was called to the wooden door-hinges.

Rupp says that they all observed great abstemiousness in their diet; they were vegetarians, and submitted to many privations and to a rigid discipline exerted over them by a somewhat austere spiritual father.

Peter Miller himself says that he stood under Beissel's direction for thirty years, and that it

* The Chronicle tells us that once, in Beissel's absence, a costly feather bed was brought into his sleeping-room. He made use of it one night, but sent it away afterward,—and not even in dying could be brought to give up the sleeping-bench (der Schlafbanck).

was as severe as any related in the Roman Church (but this sounds exaggerated).

In the Brother- and Sister-houses, it has been stated that six dormitories surrounded a common room in which the members of each subdivision pursued their respective employments. "Each dormitory was hardly large enough to contain a cot, a closet, and an hour-glass."*

Of the industries established at Ephrata, one of Peter Miller's letters gives us a good idea. He complains, as before mentioned, of Eckerlin's obliging them to interfere so far in worldly things, and of money's being put out at interest.

He adds that they erected a grist-mill, with three pairs of stones; a saw-mill, paper-mill, oil-mill, and fulling-mill; had besides three wagons with proper teams, a printing-office, and sundry other trades.

He adds, " Our president [by whom he means Beissel] never meddled with temporal things."

Mr. Rupp (who cites the Life of Rittenhouse)

---

* In Carey's Museum for 1789, will be found a letter from a British officer to the editor of the Edinburgh Magazine, whence it appears that at that time, 1786, a rug was laid upon the sleeping-bench. The writer says that each brother had a cell, with a closet adjoining; that the smallness of the rooms was very disagreeable, and that they were not clean. The churches were clean and neat, but perfectly unadorned, except by some German texts. The house " occupied by the nuns" was uniformly clean, and the cells were in excellent order. (Some of the statements of this writer appear very loose.)

says that the women were employed in spinning, knitting, sewing, making paper lanterns and other toys. A room was set apart for ornamental writing, called "Das Schreibzimmer," and "several Sisters," it has been said, devoted their whole attention to this labor, as well as to transcribing the writings of the founder of the society; thus multiplying copies before they had a press.

But the press appears to have been early established, and it was the second German one in our State. It has been stated that Miller was at one time the printer.*

Among the books published at Ephrata, were some of Beissel's, who had adopted the title, it seems, of Peaceful (Friedsam). One of their publications was a collection of hymns, and was entitled "The Song of the Solitary and Abandoned Turtle Dove, namely, the Christian Church, ... by a Peaceful Pilgrim traveling towards Quiet Eternity." Ephrata, from the press of the Fraternity, 1747. 500 pages, quarto.†

---

* At Ephrata, in the winter of 1872, I was told that Miller was once met, as he was taking a load of paper from the mill to the press, by a certain man named Widman. This Widman, according to tradition, had been a vestryman in Miller's former church. "Is this the way they treat you," said Widman, "harnessing you up to a wheelbarrow?" and he spit in Miller's face.

Allusion will be made hereafter to the traditionary tale of Miller and Widman.

† Of one of the collections of hymns published at Ephrata,

Beissel also wrote a Dissertation on Man's Fall, which Miller seems to have much admired. He says (1790), "When, in the late war, a marquis from Milan, in Italy, lodged a night in our convent, I presented to him the said dissertation, and desired him to publish it at home, and dedicate it to his Holiness," etc.

In 1748, a stupendous book was published by the society at Ephrata. It is the Martyr's Mirror, in folio, of which copies may be seen at the libraries of the Pennsylvania Historical Society, and of the German Society, in Philadelphia.

The Chronicon Ephratense, or Ephrata Chronicle, so often alluded to in this article, was also from their press, but was published thirty-eight years later.

It contains the life of the venerable "Father in Christ, Peaceful Godright (Gottrecht), late founder and *Vorsteher* of the Spiritual Order of the Solitary (Einsamen) in Ephrata, collected by Brothers Lamech and Agrippa." I have heard within this year of three copies still extant,—one in Lancaster County, one in Montgomery, and one in the Library of the Historical Society at

---

Fahnestock says that four hundred and forty-one were written by Beissel, seventy-three by the Brethren in the cloister, one hundred by the single Sisters, and one hundred and twelve by the out-door members.

Endress speaks in unfavorable terms of the literary merits of some of the Ephrata hymns.

Philadelphia. The last I have been allowed to consult.

In speaking of the industries practiced at Ephrata, it may be permitted to include music. Beissel is said to have been an excellent musician and composer. "There was another transcribing-room," says Fahnestock, "appropriated to copying music. Hundreds of volumes, each containing five or six hundred pieces, were transferred from book to book, with as much accuracy, and almost as much neatness, as if done with a graver."

In composing music, Beissel is said to have taken his style from nature. "The singing is the Æolian harp harmonized. . . . Their music is set in four, six, and eight parts."

Morgan Edwards* (as cited in Day's Historical Collections) says, "Their singing is charming,—partly owing to the pleasantness of their voices, the variety of parts they carry on together, and the devout manner of performance." This style of singing is said by Rupp (1844) to be entirely lost at Ephrata, but to be preserved in a measure at Snow Hill, in Franklin County. Fahnestock, who was himself a Seventh-Day Baptist (or Siebtaeger), gives a very enthusiastic

---

* " Materials towards a History of the American Baptists." 1770.

account of the singing at Snow Hill. It may be found in Day's Historical Collections, article "Franklin County."*

In addition to the various industries which claimed the attention of the community, there must not be forgotten the care of their landed estate. It has been said that they bought about two hundred and fifty acres of land.†

A very large tract was once offered to them by one of the Penns, but they refused it. (I was told at Ephrata that they were "afraid they would get too vain.")

Count Zinzendorf, the celebrated Moravian

---

* Dr. Fahnestock resided for awhile in the latter part of his life in the Sister-house, at Ephrata. Here Mr. Rupp, the historian, visited him. Rev. Mr. Shrigley, librarian of the Pennsylvania Historical Society, who visited Ephrata, has spoken to me of Fahnestock's venerable appearance.

† In after-years they seem to have been much troubled by litigation. Dr. Fahnestock says that they considered contention with arms, and at law, unchristian; but that they unfortunately had to defend themselves often in courts of justice. To set an example of forbearance and Christian meekness, they suffered themselves for a long time to be plundered, until forbearance was no longer a virtue. He says (Hazard's Register, 1835) that the society is just escaping from heavy embarrassments which they incurred in defending themselves from the aggressions of their neighbors.

The British officer, whose statement was published as early as 1789, speaks of Peter Miller as often engaged in litigation.

In a recent work (Belcher's History of Religious Denominations, 1854), the Seventh-Day Baptists at Ephrata are said to possess about one hundred and forty acres.

bishop, came to Pennsylvania in 1741. At one time he visited Ephrata, and was entertained in the convent, where his friendly behavior was very agreeable to the Brothers. (We can suppose that Miller, and Eckerlin, who was not yet deposed, were men fit to entertain him.) He also expressed a wish to see Beissel. This was made known to the latter, who answered, after a little reflection, that = = = =* was no wonder to him, but if he himself were a wonder to him (Zinzendorf), he must come to him (to Beissel's house ?).

Zinzendorf was now in doubt what to do, but he turned away and left without seeing the Father (Vorsteher).

The Chronicle adds that thus did two great lights of the church meet as on the threshold, and yet neither ever saw the other in his life.

At a later date, the Moravians erected Brother- and Sister-houses at Litiz, in our county, and elsewhere, but they were not monastic institutions.†

Is it possible that the idea of erecting those

---

* = = = = (printed thus in the Chronicle). Were they ashamed to insert the name Zinzendorf, or his title, "The Ordinary"?

† It does not appear that the Celibates at Ephrata were bound by vows. All our other German Baptists are conscientiously opposed to oaths.

houses originated from this visit of their great leader to Ephrata?

Dissension arose at one time between some of the Brethren (apparently secular brothers) and Count Zinzendorf, at a conference held by the latter at Oley, now in Berks County. Zinzendorf seems to have desired to unite some of the sects with which Pennsylvania was so well supplied. But the Solitary Brethren (of Ephrata) were so suspicious of the thing that they would no longer unite with it. They had prepared a writing upon Marriage,—how far it is from God, and that it was only a praiseworthy ordinance of nature. This they presented, whereupon there arose a violent conflict in words.

The Ordinarius (Zinzendorf) said that he was by no means pleased with this paper; his marriage had not such a beginning; his marriage stood higher than the solitary life in Ephrata. The Ephrata delegates strove to make all right again, and spoke of families in their Society who had many children. (See Chronicle.)

But Zinzendorf left his seat as chairman, . . . and at last the conference came to an end, all present being displeased.*

---

* A writer in the Chronicle speaks of being at one of the Count's conferences, where there were Mennonites, Separatists, and Baptists.

But when he came home, he told the *Vorsteher* that he re-

About this date (or about 1740) took place the formation of the Sabbath-school, by Ludwig Hoecker, called Brother Obed. He was a teacher in the secular school at Ephrata,—a school which seems to have enjoyed considerable reputation. The Sabbath-school (held on Saturday afternoon) is said to have been kept up over thirty years. This was begun long before the present Sunday-school system was introduced by Robert Raikes.*—(American Cyclopædia, article "Dunkers.") .

Not long after the visit of Zinzendorf, or about 1745, occurred the deposition of Eckerlin, the Prior Onesimus.

In one of his letters, Miller says (1790), " Remember, we have lost our first prior and the

---

garded the Count's conference as a snare to bring simple awakened souls again into infant-baptism and church-going. '

Then they held a council, and resolved to have a yearly conference of their own.

The above expression—infant-baptism and church-going—sounds so much like the account of the Baptist or Anabaptist persecutions narrated in the Martyr-book, that we might almost conclude that the Dunkers had a direct connection with the Anabaptists, instead of originating among the Pietists. But it will be remembered that the Ephrata Dunkers had published an edition of the great Martyr-book, and it is most probable that some of them were familiar with it. Still, there may have been among the Pietists some who were or had been Baptists.

* Near the close of this sketch mention is made of " Hoeckers a Creveld." Perhaps Ludwig belonged to the same family.

Sisters their first mother . . . . because they
stood in self-elevation, and did govern despotic-
ally ;" and adds, "The desire to govern is the
last thing which dies within a man."

(It seems probable that Eckerlin has not received sufficient credit for the pecuniary success
of the infant community.)

Some ten years after this occurrence (or in
1755), began the old French and Indian war.

Fahnestock tells us that the doors of the cloister, including the chapels, etc., were opened as
a refuge for the inhabitants of Tulpehocken and
Paxton* settlements, which were then the fron-
tiers, to protect the people from the incursions
of the hostile Indians. He adds that all these
refugees were received and kept by the Society
during the period of alarm and danger. Upon
hearing of which, a company of infantry was
despatched by the royal government from Philadelphia to protect Ephrata.

But why, we might ask, did these people seek
refuge in a community of non-combatants? The
question bears upon the yet unsettled contro-
versy, as to whether the men of peace or the
men of war were nearer† right in their dealings
with the savages.

---

* Paxton Township is now Dauphin County. (See Day.)
The Paxton church was three miles east of Harrisburg.

† The Mennonites, Moravians, and Quakers were peaceably
disposed towards the Indians, but the Presbyterians from the

Beissel died in the year 1768, or about thirty years after the establishment of the cloister.

Upon his tombstone was placed, in German, this inscription:

"Here rests a Birth of the love of God, Peaceful, a Solitary, but who afterward became a Superintendent of the Solitary Community of Christ in and around Ephrata: born in Oberbach in the Palatinate, and named Conrad Beissel.

"He fell asleep the 6th of July, A.D. 1768: of his spiritual life 52, but of his natural one, 77 years and 4 months."

The character of Beissel is thus spoken of by Mr. Endress:

"He appears to me to have been a man possessed of a considerable degree of the spirit of rule; his mind bent from the beginning upon the acquirement of authority, power and ascendency." For ourselves, we have just seen

---

north of Ireland, who were settled at Paxton, felt a deadly animosity against them, and, as Day says, against the peaceful Moravians and Quakers, who wished to protect the Indians, as the Paxton men thought, at the expense of the lives of the settlers. The Paxton Rangers were commanded by the Presbyterian minister, the Rev. Colonel Elder.

Mr. Elder seems to have opposed the massacre of the Indians at Lancaster by the "Paxton boys."

"No historian," says Day, "ought to excuse or justify the murders at Lancaster and Conestoga. . . . They must ever remain . . . dark and bloody spots in our provincial history."

how he received the Count Zinzendorf, a religious nobleman, who had crossed the ocean, and come, as it were, to his threshold.

Mr. Endress further says,—

"Beissel, good or bad, lived and died the master-spirit of the brotherhood. With him it sank into decay."

The British officer who wrote in 1786 (?), eighteen years after Beissel's death, gives the number of the celibates as seven men and five women.

I do not consider him good authority; but if the numbers were so much reduced from those of 1740, it seems probable that they had begun to decline before the decease of Beissel.*

Eighteen years after Beissel's death, was published at Ephrata the Chronicle of which I have so often spoken, giving an account of his life. Beissel was succeeded by Peter Miller.

Miller was sixty-five when our Revolutionary war broke out, and had been the leader at Ephrata seven years.

Fahnestock says that after the battle of Brandywine "the whole establishment was opened to receive the wounded Americans, great numbers of whom (Rupp says four or five hundred) were brought here in wagons a distance of more

---

* See Carey's American Museum.

than forty miles, and one hundred and fifty of whom died and are buried on Mt. Zion."*

It is also narrated that before the battle of Germantown, a quantity of unbound books were seized at Ephrata by some of our soldiers, in order to make cartridges. "An embargo," says Miller, "was laid on all our printed paper, so that for a time we could not sell any printed book." (See Carey's American Museum.)

A story has appeared in print, and not always in the same manner, about Miller's going to General Washington and receiving from him a pardon for his old enemy Widman, who was condemned to die.

This story Mr. Rupp thinks is based upon tradition; one version has been told in a glowing manner, and is attributed to Dr. Fahnestock. It runs thus. On the breaking out of the Revolution, Committees of Safety were formed in different districts to support our cause. At the head of the Lancaster County Committee was Michael Widman, who kept a public house, and who had been a vestryman in the Reformed Church. This church Miller had left when he joined the Baptists. He persecuted Miller to a shameful extent, even spitting in his face when he met him.

---

* An insignificant hill overlooking the meadow where the Brother- and Sister-houses now stand.

Widman was at first bold and active in the cause of Independence, but he became discouraged, and resolved to go to Philadelphia and conciliate General Howe, the British commander, who then held that city. Howe, however, declined his services,* but gave orders to see him safely beyond the British outposts.

His treasonable intentions having become known to the Americans, he was arrested and taken to the nearest block-house, at the Turk's Head, now Westchester; was tried by court-martial, and sentenced to be hung.

Peter Miller, hearing of his arrest, went to General Washington and pleaded for mercy towards him. The general answered that the state of public affairs was such as to make it necessary that renegades should suffer, "otherwise I should most cheerfully release your friend."

"Friend!" exclaimed Miller: "he is my worst enemy,—my incessant reviler."

Said the general, "My dear friend, I thank you for this example of Christian charity!" and he granted Miller's petition.

It is not necessary for me to go further, and describe the scene of Miller's arriving upon the ground with the pardon just as Widman was to be hung, nor the subsequent proceedings there, for I am quite sure that they did not take place.

---

* A remarkable statement.

The evidence to this effect is found in the Pennsylvania Archives, vol. ix., where Peter Miller writes to Secretary Matlack, interceding (apparently) for a man named Rein.

Miller says, "I have thought his case was similar to Michael Wittman's, who received pardon without a previous trial."

The secretary replies (1781), "Witman did not receive a pardon previous to a surrender."

Thus it seems that the story of Widman's trial by court-martial is also•wrong. That his property was confiscated, as I was lately told at Ephrata, I have no reason to doubt, as the Colonial Records, vol. xii., show that in council, in 1779, it was resolved that the agents for forfeited estates should sell that of Michael Wittman, subject to a certain claim.*

At Ephrata, during the past winter, I stood in the loft of the Brother-house beside a great chimney of wood and clay, and was told that here Widman had been hidden. Whether he actually concealed himself in the Brother-house, as has been narrated, I do not find that history declares.

At a subsequent date, 1783, we find in the Pennsylvania Archives, vol. ix., that Miller intercedes for certain Mennonites who had been

---

* The different modes of spelling the above name will not surprise those who are familiar with our Pennsylvania German names.

fined for not apprehending British deserters; the Mennonites not being permitted by their principles to do so.

Does this mean deserters from ourselves to the British?—who were, as deserters, liable to the punishment of death? a punishment which the Mennonites, as non-resistants, could not inflict.

Certain letters of Peter Miller, published in Hazard's Register, and of which I have made considerable use, were written at an advanced age,—eighty or thereabout. He says in one of them (Dec., 1790), "Age, infirmity, and defect in sight are causes that the letter wants more perspicuity, for which I beg pardon."

He died about six years after, having lived some sixty years a member of the community at Ephrata.

Upon his tombstone was placed this inscription in German:

"Here lies buried Peter Miller, born in Ober-ampt Lautern, in the Palatinate (Chur-Pfalz); came as a Reformed preacher to America in the year 1730; was baptized by the Community at Ephrata in the year 1735, and named Brother Jaebez; also he was afterward a preacher (*Lehrer*) until his end. He fell asleep the 25th of September, 1796, at the age of eighty-six years and nine months."

In the plain upon the banks of the Cocalico

still stand the Brother- and Sister-houses,* and, I was told in 1872, the houses of Conrad Beissel and of Peter Miller.

But the society is feeble in numbers, and the buildings are going to decay. They are still, however, occupied, or partly so. Several women live here. Some of these were never married, but the majority are widows; and not all of them are members of the Baptist congregation. Nor are the voices of children wanting.

The last celibate brother died some forty years ago. One, indeed, has been here since, but, as I was told, " he did not like it," and went to the more flourishing community of Snow Hill, in Franklin County.

The little Ephrata association (which still owns a farm), instead of supporting its unmarried members, now furnishes to them only house-rent, fuel, and flour. The printing-press long since ceased from its labors, and many of the other industrial pursuits have declined.

No longer do the unmarried or celibate members own all the property, but it is now vested in all who belong to the meeting, single and married, and is in the hands of trustees. The income is, I presume, but small.

The unmarried members wear our usual dress, and none are strictly recluse.

---

* Not the buildings first erected.

15*

Formerly a large room or chapel was connected with the Brother-house. It was furnished with galleries, where sat the sisters, while the brethren occupied the floor below. This building, I am told, is not standing. In the smaller room or chapel (Saal) connected with the Sister-house, about twenty people meet on the Seventh day for public worship. But among all these changes the German language still remains! All the services that I heard while attending here in February of 1872, were in that tongue, except two hymns at the close. We must not suppose that this language is employed because the members are natives of Germany. One or two may be, but the preacher's father or grandfather came to this country when a boy.

Around the meeting-room are hung charts or sheets of grayish paper, containing German verses in ornamental writing, the ancient labors of the celibates, or perhaps of the sisters alone. One small chart here is said to represent the three heavens, and to contain three hundred figures in Capuchin dress, with harps in their hands, and two hundred archangels.

But for these old labors in pen and ink, the chapel is as plain as a Quaker meeting-house, and is kept beautifully clean.*

---

* It may be observed how nearly this description of the chapel agrees with that given by the British officer of the one he visited here some eighty-five years ago.

Opening out of it is a kitchen, furnished with the apparatus for cooking and serving the simple repasts of the love-feasts.

Among these Baptists, love-feasts are held not only, as I understand, in a similar manner to the other Dunkers, but upon funeral occasions,— a short period after the interment of a brother or sister.

Rupp speaks of their eating lamb and mutton at their Paschal feasts. In the old monastic time, it was only at love-feasts that the celibate Brothers and Sisters met.

Here was I shown a wooden goblet made by the brethren for the Communion. It has been said that they preferred to use such, even after more costly ones had been given to them.

After attending the religious services in the chapel, three or four of us—strangers—were supplied with dinner in the Brother-house, at a neat and well-filled table.*

I afterward sat for an hour in the neat and comfortable apartment of Sister —— in the Sister-house. Here she has lived twenty-two years, and, though now much advanced in life, has not that appearance. She seemed lovely, and, I was told, had not been unsought.

---

* Fahnestock says that, like some dilapidated castles, Ephrata yet contains many habitable and comfortable apartments. The Brother- and Sister-houses, etc., form but a small part of the modern village of Ephrata.

One of her brothers has been thirty-three years at the Snow Hill community.

Sister —— produced for me a white cotton over-dress, such as was formerly worn by the Sisters. It was a cap or cowl, with long pieces hanging down in front and behind nearly to the feet; and, if I remember it right, not of the pattern described in the Chronicle. But fashions change in fifty to a hundred years.

Sister —— also showed me some verses recently written or copied by one of the brethren at Snow Hill. They were in German, of which I offer an unrhymed version :

"Oh divine life, ornament of virginity !
How art thou despised by all men here below!
And yet art a branch from the heavenly throne,
And borne by the virgin Son of God."

I was surprised to find such prominence still given to the idea of the merits of celibacy, for I had not then seen the *Chronicon Ephratense.*

One object which especially attracted my attention was an upright clock, which stood in the room of Sister ——, and which was kept in nice order. It was somewhat smaller than the high clocks that were common forty or fifty years ago.

All that I heard of its history was that it had come from Germany. It had four weights suspended on chains. Above the dial-plate hovered two little angels, apparently made of lead, one on either side of a small disk, which bore the inscription "Hoeckers a Creveld,"—as I interpret, made by the Hoeckers at Crefeld. Crefeld,—historic town! Here then was a relic of it, and standing quite disregarded,—it was only an old German clock.

When the Dunkers were persecuted in Europe, soon after their establishment, some of them took refuge in Crefeld, in the duchy of Cleves.

I have lately read that in Crefeld, Mühlheim, etc., William Penn and others gained adherents to the doctrine of the Quakers.*

We also find in the American Cyclopædia that at Crefeld (German, Krefeld), a colony of Huguenot refugees in the seventeenth century introduced the manufacture of silk. The town is now in Rhenish Prussia (says the Cyclopædia). Dunkers, Quakers, Huguenots, fleeing perhaps from France when Louis XIV. revoked that edict of Nantes, which had so long protected them!

Who were the Heckers, or who was the Hoecker, that made this old clock? Who bought it in historic Crefeld? Who brought it from Europe, got it up into Lancaster County, and lodged it in the monastery or nunnery at Ephrata? What, if anything, had Ludwig Hoecker or Brother Obed to do with it? What tales could it not

---

* See article "Francis Daniel Pastorius," by Dr. Seidensticker, in the *Penn Monthly*, January and February, 1872.

tell! But it is well cared for in the comfortable apartment of the kindly sister.

The Snow-Hill settlement, I presume, is named from the family of Snowberger (Schneeberger?), one of whom endowed the society. It is situated at Antietam, Franklin County, Pennsylvania; where a large farm belongs to "the nunnery" (to quote an expression that I heard at Ephrata). There were, until lately, five Sisters and four brothers at Antietam, but one of the Brethren recently died.

The Brethren have sufficient occupation in taking care of their property; the Sisters keep house, eating in the same apartment at the same time with the Brothers. Under these circumstances I could imagine the comfort and order of the establishment, and think of the Brothers and Sisters meeting in a cool and shaded dining-room. What question then should I be likely to ask? This one: "Do they never marry?"

I was told that marriages between the Brothers and Sisters are not unknown; but I also understood that such a thing is considered backsliding.

Persons thus married remain members of the church, but must leave the community, and find support elsewhere.*

---

* Mr. Endress tells us that with many of the single Brethren and Sisters at Ephrata, the mystical idea of the union with Christ was evidently used to gratify one of the strongest natural affections of the human heart. "The Redeemer was their

In an article by Redmond Conyngham (Haz. Reg., vol. v.) will be found the statement that the "President of the Dunkers" says,—

"We deny eternal punishment; those souls who become sensible of God's great goodness and clemency, and acknowledge his lawful authority, ... and that Christ is the only true Son of God, are received into happiness; but those who continue obstinate are kept in darkness until the Great Day, when light will make all happy." According to Dr. Fahnestock, however, the idea of a universal restoration, which existed in the early days, is not now publicly taught.

The observance of the seventh day as a Sabbath must always be onerous, in a community like ours. Hired people are not required by the Siebentaeger (or Seventh-day men) to work on Saturday; and, unless of their own persuasion, will not work on Sunday.

It has been said that the customs at Ephrata resembled the Judaic ones; and Endress says

---

bridegroom or bride. . . . He was the little infant they carried under their hearts, the dear little lamb they dandled on their laps."

He adds that this at least was found much more among the single than among those whose affections were consecrated in a conjugal life. "The powers of human nature would evince their authority." "According to Sangmeister, some sank under the unceasing struggle." See Hazard's Register, 1830.

that they consider baptism similar to purification in the Mosaic law,—as a rite which may be repeated from time to time when the believer has become defiled by the world, and would again renew his union with Christ.

But Miller says (1790), "Our standard is the New Testament."*

Fahnestock says that they do not approve of paying their ministers; and it seems that the women, or at least the single Sisters, are at liberty to speak in religious meetings.

In the correspondence of one of our Lancaster papers of 1871, there was given the following account: "Ephrata, May 21.—The Society of the Seventh-Day Baptists held their semi-annual love-feast yesterday, when one new member was added to the Society by immersion. In the evening the solemn feast of the Lord's Supper was celebrated, the occasion attracting a large concourse of people,—only about half of whom could obtain seats. The conduct of a number of persons on the outside was a disgrace to an intelligent community."

The article also mentions preachers as present from Bedford, Franklin, and Somerset Counties. However, the whole number of the Seventh-Day German Baptists, in our State, is very small.

---

* Upon this subject of the New Testament as a creed, etc., all or nearly all our German Baptist sects seem to unite.

[Note.—Since this article was written, the author has heard what is the present location of the bell which was ordered from Europe by Eckerlin,—Brother Onesimus,—and which caused so much dissension in the little Ephrata Community when it arrived in the year 1745.

This bell was sold, as has been before stated, to the Lutherans of Lancaster. It was long in use upon Trinity Lutheran Church, but was afterwards sold to one of the fire-engine or hose companies of Lancaster, and is still in use, and in good preservation, bearing upon it the Latin inscription, with the name of the "reverend man" Onesimus.

Is there an older bell in use upon this continent?]

16

A FRIEND.

About twenty miles from the State line that divides Maryland and Pennsylvania, there stands, in the latter State, a retired farm-house, which was erected more than fifty years ago by Samuel Wilson, a Quaker of Quakers.

His was a character so rare in its quaintness and its nobility, that it might serve as a theme for a pen more practiced and more skillful than the one that now essays to portray it.

Samuel Wilson was by nature romantic. When comparatively young, he made a pedestrian tour to the Falls of Niagara, stopping upon his return journey, and hiring with a farmer to recruit his exhausted funds; and when he had passed his grand climacteric, the enthusiasm of his friend-ship for the young, fair, and virtuous, still showed the poetic side of his character.

Veneration induced him to cherish the relics of his ancestry,—not only the genealogical tree, which traced the Wilsons back to the time of William Penn, and the marriage certificates of

(178)

his father and grandfather, according to the regular order of the Society of Friends, but such more humble and familiar heirlooms as the tall eight-day clock, and the high bookcase upon a desk and chest of drawers, that had been his father's, as well as the strong kitchen-chairs and extremely heavy fire-irons of his grandfather.

To this day there stands at the end of the barn, near the Wilson farm-house, a stone taken from one of the buildings erected by Samuel's father, and preserved as an heirloom. Upon it the great-grandchildren read nearly the following inscription :

"James Wilson, ejus manus scripsit. Deborah Wilson, 5 mo. 23d, 1757."

Samuel Wilson, having been trained from his earliest years to that plainness of speech in which the Discipline requires that Friends bring up those under their care, not only discarded in speaking the simple titles in use in common conversation, but did not himself desire to be addressed as Mr. Wilson.

A colored woman, the wife of one of his tenants, said that he refused to answer her when she thus spoke to him.

A pleasant euphemism was generally employed by these people in addressing him. He and his wife were "Uncle Samuel" and "Aunt Anna" to their numerous dependents.

The apparel of Samuel and Anna was of the

strict pattern of their own religious sect. To employ a figure of speech, it was the " weddinggarment," without which, at that time and place, they would not have become elders in their society, and thus been entitled to sit with ministers, etc., upon the rising seats that faced the rest of the meeting. But the plainness of Uncle Samuel was not limited to the fashion of his own garments.

When Aunt Anna had made for her son a suit of domestic cloth, dyed brown with the hulls of the black walnut, and had arrayed him in his new clothes, of which the trousers were made roomy behind,—or, as the humorist says, " baggy in the reverse,"—she looked upon him with maternal pride and fondness, and exclaimed, " There's my son !"

For this ejaculation she was not only reproved at the time by her husband, but in after-years, whenever he heard her, as he thought, thus fostering in the mind of their dear child pride in external appearance, he repeated the expression, " There's my son !" which saying conveyed a volume of reproof.

From this and other circumstances of the kind, it may be supposed that Friend Wilson was a cold or bitter ascetic. But he possessed a vein of humor, and could be gently and pleasantly rallied when he seemed to run into extremes. But, though his intellect was good, the moral sentiments predominated in his character. His head was lofty and arched.

His wants were very few; he possessed an ample competence, and he had no ambition to enter upon the fatiguing chase after riches. He disliked acquisitive men as much as the latter despised him. "I want so little for myself," he said, "I think that I might be allowed to give something away."

Sometimes—but rarely—a little abruptness was seen in his behavior. He had the manners of a gentleman by birth,—tender and true, open to melting charity, thinking humbly of himself, and respecting others.

The vein of humor to which I have alluded prompted the reply which he made on a certain occasion to a mechanic or laboring-man employed in his own family. In this section of Lancaster County. the farming population is composed principally of a laborious and in some respects a humble-minded people, who sit at table and eat with their hired people of both sexes.

The same custom was pursued by Samuel and Anna; but, as their hired people were mostly colored, they sometimes offended the prejudices or tastes of many who were not accustomed to this equality of treatment, which was maintained by several families of Friends. The white hired man to whom I have alluded, when he perceived

16*

who were seated at the table, hesitated or refused
to sit down among them. As soon as Samuel was
conscious of the difficulty, for which, indeed, his
mind was not unprepared, he thus spoke aloud
to his wife: " Anna, will thee set a plate at that
other table for this stranger ? He does not want
to sit down with us." And his request was
quietly obeyed. The man who was thus set apart
probably became tired of this peculiar seclusion,
for he did not stay long at the Quaker homestead.

I think that Samuel was also in a humorous
mood when he called that unpretending instru-
ment, the accordeon,—from which his daughter-
in-law was striving one evening to draw forth
musical sounds,—" Mary's fiddle."   .

Indeed, he left the house and went to call upon
a neighbor, so greatly did he partake of that
prejudice which was felt by most Friends against
music.

The Discipline asks whether Friends are punc-
tual to their promises; and (to quote a very
different work) Fielding tells us that Squire All-
worthy was not only careful to keep his greater
engagements, but remembered also his promises
to visit his friends.

Anna Wilson on one occasion having thought-
lessly made such a promise,—as, indeed, those
in society frequently do when their friends say,
" Come and see us,"—was often reminded of it
in after-years by her husband. When he heard

her lightly accepting such invitations, he would
humorously reprove her by saying in private,
" When is thee going to see Benjamin Smith ?"
—the neighbor to whom the ancient promise was
still unfulfilled.

The hospitality which the Scriptures enjoin
was practiced to a remarkable degree by Samuel
and Anna. It has always been customary in
their Religious Society to entertain Friends who
come from a distance to attend meetings, and
those traveling as preachers, etc. But the Wilson
homestead was a place of rest and entertainment
for many more than these. It stood not far from
the great highway laid out by William Penn
from Philadelphia westward, and here called the
" Old Road." Friends traveling westward in
their own conveyance would stop and refresh
themselves and their horses at the hospitable
mansion, and would further say to their own
friends, " Thee'd better stop at Samuel Wilson's.
Tell him I told thee to stop." But a further and
greater extent of hospitality I shall mention
hereafter.

The Discipline asks whether Friends are careful to keep those under their charge from pernicious books and from the corrupt conversation
of the world; and I have heard that Samuel
Wilson was grieved when his son began to go to
the post-office and take out newspapers. Hith-
erto the principal periodical that came to the

house was *The Genius of Universal Emancipation,* a little paper issued by that pioneer, Benjamin Lundy, who was born and reared in the Society of Friends. It does not appear, however, that the class of publications brought from the little village post-office to the retired farm-house were of the class usually called pernicious. They were *The Liberator, The Emancipator,* and others of the same class.

Samuel himself became interested in them, but never to the exclusion of the "Friends' Miscellany," a little set of volumes containing religious anecdotes of Friends. These volumes were by him highly prized and frequently read.

It has been said that he was a humorist; and perhaps he was partly jesting when he suggested that his infant grand-daughter should be named Tabitha. The mother of the little one, on her part, brought forward the name Helen.

"He-len!" the grandfather broke out in reply; "does thee know who *she* was ?" thus expressing his antipathy to the character of the notorious beauty of Greece. He did not insist, however, on endowing the precious newly-born infant with that peculiar name, which is by interpretation Dorcas, the name of her who, in apostolic times, was full of good works and alms-deeds.

Friend Wilson shared the Quaker disregard for the great holidays of the Church. To the colored people who surrounded him, who had been brought up at the South, where Christmas is so great á festival,—where it was so great a holiday for them especially,—it must have been a sombre change to live in a family where the day passed nearly like other working-days. One of the colored men, however, who had started at the time of the great festival to *take 'Christmas*, was seen, before long, coming back; "for," said he, "Massa Wilson don't 'prove on't no-how."

Among the lesser peculiarities of Samuel Wilson was his objection to having his picture taken,—an objection, however, which is felt to this day by some strict people belonging to other religious societies, but probably on somewhat different grounds.

One who warmly loved and greatly respected Friend Wilson took him once to the rooms of an eminent daguerreotypist, hoping that while he engaged the venerable man in looking at the objects around the room, the artist might be able to catch a likeness. But Samuel suspected some artifice, and no picture was taken. Some time after, however, the perseverance of his friend was rewarded by obtaining an excellent oil-painting of the aged man, from whom a reluctant consent to sit for his likeness had at length been obtained. It was remarked, however, that the expression of the face in the painting was sorrowful, as if the honorable man was grieved at complying with a custom which he had long stigmatized as idolatrous,—as idolatry of the perishing body.

Although at the time of the great division in the Society of Friends Samuel Wilson had decidedly taken the part of Elias Hicks, yet was he seldom or never heard to discuss those questions of dogmatic theology which some have thought were involved in that contest.

Samuel probably held, with many others of his Society, that the highest and surest guide which man possesses here is that Light which has been said to illumine every man that comes into the world; that next in importance is a rightly inspired gospel ministry, and afterward the Scriptures of truth. One evening, when certain mechanics in his employ were resting from their labors in the old-fashioned kitchen, he fell into conversation with them on matters of religion, and shocked one of his family, as he entered the sitting-room, by a sudden declaration of opinion. It was probably the uncommon warmth of his manner which produced this effect, quite as much as or more than the words that he spoke, which were about as follows : " There's no use talking about it; the only religion in the world that's worth anything is what makes men do what is right and leave off doing what is wrong."

As far as was possible for one with so much fearless independence of thought and action,

Samuel Wilson maintained the testimony of Friends against war. Not only did he suffer his corn to be seized in the field rather than pay voluntarily the military taxes of the last war with Great Britain, but he went to what may appear to some a laughable extreme, in forbidding his young son's going to the turnpike to see the grand procession which was passing near their house, escorting General Lafayette on his last visit to this country. He was not, however, alone in this. I have heard of other decided Friends who declined to swell the ovation to a man who was especially distinguished as a military hero. But we shall see hereafter that Friend Wilson met with circumstances which tried his non-resistant opinions further than they would bear.

The distinctive trait of his character, however, —that trait which made him exceptional,—was his attachment to the people of color. It was in entertaining fugitives from slavery that he showed the wide hospitality already referred to; and in this active benevolence he was excelled by few in our country. He inherited from his father this love of man; but I have imagined that the hostility to slavery was made broad and deep in his soul by removing, with the rest of his family, in his youth, from Pennsylvania into Delaware, and seeing the bondage which was suffered by colored people in the latter State contrasted with what he had seen in the former. Be that as it may, no sooner was he a householder than his door was ever open to those who were escaping from the South, coming by stealth and in darkness, having traveled in the Slave States from the house of one free negro to another, and in Pennsylvania from Quaker to Quaker, until in later times the hostility to slavery increased in our community so far that others became agents of this underground railroad, and other routes were opened.

When the Wilson family came down in the morning, they saw standing around these strange sable or yellow travelers (" strangers," they were called in the family), who, having arrived during the night, had been received by some wakeful member of the household.

What feelings filled the hearts of the exiles! Alone, at times, having left all that they had ever loved of persons or of places, fearful, tired, foot-sore, throwing themselves upon the charity and the honor of a man unknown to them save by name and the direction which they had received to him, as one trustworthy.

Sometimes they came clothed in the undyed woolen cloth that showed so plainly to one experienced in the matter the region of its manufacture,—the heavy, strong cloth which had delighted the wearer's heart when he received the annual Christmas suit with which his master furnished him, but which was now too peculiar and too striking for him to safely wear. Women and children came too, and sometimes in considerable numbers.

When they had eaten and partaken of the necessary repose, they would communicate to Friend Wilson, in a secure situation, some particulars of their former history, especially the names and residences of the masters from whom they had escaped.

Some years after he had begun to entertain these strangers, Friend Wilson commenced a written record of those who came to him, and whence and from whom they had escaped. This list is estimated to have finally contained between five and six hundred names.

The next care was to bestow new titles upon the fugitives, that they might never be known by their former names to the pursuer and the betrayer.

From what has been already said, it may be supposed that these names were not always selected for their euphony or æsthetic associations. One tall, finely-built yellow man, who trembled when he was questioned in the sitting-room, lest his conversation about his old home and the free wife whom he longed to have brought to him, should be overheard in the kitchen, expressed to me his dissatisfaction with his new name—*Simon.* "I never knowed anybody named that," he said. His beautiful bright wife—bright in

the *colored* sense — that is, bright-colored, or
nearly white—was secretly and safely brought to
him, and nursed him through that fatal disease
which made him of no value in the man-market,
—the market which had been the great horror of
his life. The particulars Friend Wilson collected
concerning his humble charge the venerable
man entered in his day-book, in a place specially
assigned to them. If this record were still existing, I should, perhaps, be able to tell what
name the fortunate and unfortunate Simon had
been obliged to renounce. This record, however, is lost, as I shall mention hereafter. If the
services of any of these fugitives were needed,
within-doors or without, and the master's pursuit was not supposed to be imminent, they were
detained for awhile, or perhaps became permanent residents in the neighborhood; otherwise,
they were forwarded at night to Friends living
nearer Philadelphia. Of these, two other families
willing to receive the poor exiles lived about
twelve miles farther on.

The house and farm were generally pretty
well stocked with colored people, who were a
wonder to the neighbors of the Wilson family;
for these were in a great measure "Pennsylvania
Dutch,"—a people anxious to do as much work
with their own hands and by the hands of their
own family as possible, in order to avoid expense.
It is a remarkable circumstance that, although

Samuel Wilson during thirty years or more entertained the humble strangers, and although he received so large a number, only one of them was seized upon his "plantation" and taken back to slavery. This was owing partly to the secluded situation of his house, and partly to the prudence and discretion that he exercised. "He was crafty," it has been said.

Neither did he suffer any legal expenses, such as lawsuits, from the slaveholders who came in pursuit of their fleeing bondmen. Two friends who lived not far from him, and who prosecuted kidnappers, had their barns burned, and others, of whom he had knowledge, suffered great pecuniary loss in consequence of their assisting runaway slaves. He, however, limited his care to receiving, entertaining, and forwarding those who came to him in person, and never undertook any measures of offense,—any border raids, so to speak,—such as sending into Maryland and Virginia for the relatives and friends of fugitives who were still living in those States as slaves. The one person of whom I have spoken, who was recaptured from the Wilson farm, was a young girl of fifteen or sixteen. Samuel and Anna were absent from home at the time, gone on a little journey, such as they frequently took, to attend their own monthly and quarterly meetings; assisting to preserve the discipline and order of the Society of Friends. The men who came in pursuit of the young girl told her that her friends, who had run away too, had concluded to go back South again; and the poor child, under these circumstances, could hardly do anything but go with the beguilers; not, however, to find the friends whom she expected.

There was also a man who was very near being taken,—a man who had "come away," to use the brief euphemism sometimes employed in the Wilson family in speaking of fugitives from slavery. He escaped by having gone down the creek or adjacent mill-stream to set his muskrat-traps. This creek where it ran by the house was well wooded; therefore the colored man, looking up to the house, could see the white strangers without being seen himself. With what trembling did he see that they were persons whom he "knowed in Murrland," as he expressed it! However, the friendly woods sheltered him, while Samuel at the house was talking with the slaveholder or his agents,—kidnappers, as the Wilsons called them.

The men told Samuel that they had come after a runaway nigger,—black, five feet ten inches high, lost one of his front teeth, etc. To this description Friend Wilson listened in silence. I do not know what he would have done had he been directly questioned by them, for the different items suited him of the muskrats,—the man who had gone to the woods. But during Samuel's continued silence they went on to say, " He's a very ornary nigger ; no dependence to be placed on him nohow." " There is no man here," rejoined Samuel, greatly relieved, " that answers the description." " We've very good reason to think he came here," said one; " we got word very direct; reckon he's lyin' around here. Hain't there been no strange nigger here ?"

" There was a colored man here, but he has gone away; I don't know as he will ever come back again." For, from the man's protracted absence, he doubtless had some idea of his having seen his pursuers, and having sought shelter.

" Tell him that his master says that if he will only come back again, down to Baltimore county, he sha'n't be whipped, nor sold, nor nuthin', but everything shall be looked over."

" I'll tell him what you say," said Samuel, "if ever I see him again ; but," he added, regaining his accustomed independence, " I'll tell him, too, that if I was in his place I'd never go back to you again."

The men left, and under cover of the friendly night the fugitive sought a more secure hiding-place.

There was one heroic black man in whom Samuel Wilson felt an abiding interest. When Jimmy Franklin told the tale of his perilous escapes and recaptures in the States of Maryland, North and South Carolina, Georgia, and Florida,

—when he showed the shot still remaining in his legs—shot that had been fired at him as he ran, and, working through to the front, were perceived through the skin, like warts upon his legs,—the lads of the family looking and listening had their sympathies enkindled in such a manner as could never entirely die out. One of them, in after-years, was asked :

" How does thee account for that man's persistent love of freedom ? What traits of character did he possess that would account for his doing so much more than others to escape from the far South ?"

" I don't know," was the reply, in the freedom of familiar conversation. " What was the reason that Fulton invented his steamboat ? or that Bacon wrote his System ? or that Napier invented Logarithms ?

" This man was a genius,—a greater man, in his way, than those I spoke of. If he had had education, and had been placed in circumstances to draw him out, he would have been the leader in some great movement among men."

The narrative of James Franklin was taken down by a dear friend of him whom I call Samuel Wilson, but is supposed to have been burned when the mob destroyed Pennsylvania Hall.

It was in relation to these fugitives that Samuel sometimes forgot for awhile his strictly peaceful principles; for there were to be found among

the men of color those who could be induced to
betray to the pursuers their fugitive brethren,
giving such information as would lead to their
recapture; or, if they should escape this, to their
being obliged to abandon their resting-places
and to flee again for safety.

It was in talking of some such betrayer that
Samuel Wilson said to his colored friends,
" What would you do with that man, if you had
him on Mill-Creek bridge?" (a lofty structure
by which the railroad crossed the adjacent
stream,) thus hinting at a swift mode of punishment, and one that might possibly have been a
fatal one.

Though with an unskilled pen, yet have I endeavored to describe that quiet family, among
whom the fugitive-slave law of 1850 fell like a
blow. Samuel Wilson had ample opportunity
to study its provisions and its peculiarities from
the newspapers of which I have before spoken,
and from the conversation which these journals
called forth.

This horrible act gave the commissioner before
whom the colored man was tried five dollars
only if the man went free from the tribunal,
but ten dollars if he was sent into slavery. Hith-
erto, men had suffered in assisting the fugitive
to escape; now it was made a penal offense to
refuse to lend active assistance in apprehending
him.

Friend Wilson had read much of fines and imprisonment, having studied the sufferings of the people called Quakers. (Even a lady of so high a standing as she who became the wife of George Fox was not exempt from many years' imprisonment; nor from persecution at the hands of her own son.) Friend Wilson was about seventy-five years old when the fugitive-slave bill was passed. In spite of his advanced years, however, after sorrowful reflection upon it, he said to one of his household, "I have made up my mind to go to jail."

That hospitality and charity which had so long been the rule of his life he was not now prepared to forego through fear of any penalties which human laws would inflict upon him.

It was while suffering from the infirmities of advanced years, and from the solicitude which this abominable enactment had called forth, that Samuel destroyed the record which he had kept for so many years of the slaves that had taken refuge with him. This record was contained in about forty pages of his day-book, and these he cut out and burned. How would they now be prized had they not thus been lost!

Samuel Wilson saw with the prophetic eye of faith and hope, what he did not live to behold in the flesh,—the abolition of slavery. His mortal remains repose beside the Quaker meeting-house where he so long ministered as an elder. No monumental stone marks his humble resting-place; but these simple lines of mine, that portray a character so rare, may serve for an affectionate memorial.

COUSIN JEMIMA.

"WELL, Phebe, I guess thee did not expect me this afternoon. Don't get up. I will just lay my bonnet in the bedroom myself. Dinah Paddock told me thy quilt was in; so I came up as soon as I could. Laid out in orange-peel! I always did like orange-peel. Dinah's was herring-bone; and thine is filled with wool, and plims up, and shows the works, as mother used to say. I'll help thee roll before I sit down. Now then. Days are long, and we'll try to do a stroke of work, for thee's a branch quilter, I've heard say.

" Jethro Mitchell stopped to see me this morning. They got home from Ohio last week, and he says that Cousin Jemima Osborne's very bad with typhoid fever. Poor Jemima! It had been pretty much through the family, and after nursing the rest she was taken down. I almost know she has no one fit to take care of her,—only Samuel and the three boys, and maybe some hired girl that has all the housework to do.

(198)

The neighbors will be very kind, to be sure, sitting up at night; but there's been so much sickness in that country lately.

" Jemima was Uncle Brown Coffin's daughter, thee knows, who used to live down at Sandwich, on the Cape, when thee and I were girls. She always came to Nantucket to Quarterly Meeting with Uncle Brown and Aunt Judith; and folks used to say she wasn't a bit of a coof, if she *was* born on the Cape. When Samuel and she were married, they asked me and Gorham Hussey to stand up with them. Jemima looked very pretty in her lavender silk and round rosy cheeks. When meeting was over, she whispered to me that there was a wasp or bee under her neck-handkerchief that had stung her while she was saying the ceremony. But I don't think anybody perceived it, she was so quiet. Poor dear! I seem to see her now on a sick-bed and a rolling pillow.

" After my Edward died, I was so much alone that I thought I couldn't bear it any longer, and I must just get up and go to Ohio, as Samuel and 'Mima had often asked me to. I stopped on the way at Mary Cooper's at Beaver; and Mary's son was joking a little about Cousin Samuel's farming, and said he didn't quite remember whether it was two or three fences that they had to climb going from the house to the barnyard. I told him that Samuel wasn't brought up to farming; he bought land when he moved out West.

"I found Jemima a good deal altered, now that she had a grown family; but we just began where we left off,—the same friendliness and kindness. When I was in Ohio was just when the English Friends, Jonathan and Hannah Purley, were in the country. We met them at Marlborough Quarterly Meeting. We were all together at William Smith's house,—one of the neatest of places,—everything like waxwork, with three such daughters at home. How they worked to entertain Friends!

"First-day a great many world's people were at meeting on account of the strange Friends. Meeting was very full,—nearly as many out in the yard as in the house. Very weighty remarks were made by Jonathan and Hannah. She spoke to my own state:—'Leave thy widows, and let thy fatherless children trust in Me.' The meeting was disturbed some by the young babies; but we could hardly expect the mothers to stay away.

"Second-day was Quarterly Meeting. Of course the English Friends, being at William Smith's, drew a great many others. We had forty to dinner. One of William's daughters stayed in the kitchen, one waited on the table, and one sat down midway, where she could pass every.thing, and wait on the Friends. It was in the Eighth Month, and we had a bountiful table of all the good things of that time of year,—vegetables and fruits too. William was a nursery-man.

"There was a little disturbance at breakfast, William's son—a rather wild young man—making the young people laugh. We had fish,—mackerel, and little fresh fish out of the mill-dam. I sat near the middle, and heard Friend Smith at one end say to each, 'Will thee have some of the mackerel, or some of these little dam-fish?' Then young William, at the other end, spoke low to his friends: 'Will thee have some of the mackerel, or some of these dam little fish?' But most of the young women kept pretty serious countenances. When Quarterly Meeting was over, the English Friends went out to Indiana, visiting meetings and Friends' families, and I went back with Cousin Samuels'.

"I was dreadfully disappointed once. One evening Samuel and 'Mima and the rest of us were sitting round the table, and Samuel put his hand into his coat-pocket and drew out the paper and two or three letters. As he read, I noticed that one of the letters had not been opened, and caught sight of my name—Priscilla Gardner; so I put out my hand and took it. It was from sister Mary,—just as James and she were starting for California. She told me that they should stay in Pittsburgh over one night, and she hoped I should be able to meet them there and bid them a long farewell. But when I looked again at the date of the letter, and glanced at the paper that Samuel was reading, I found that my letter was ten days old. The time had gone by. Oh, dear! I walked out into the kitchen and stood by the stove, in the dark, and cried. Some one came up behind me. Of course it was Jemima. She kissed me, and waited for me to speak. I gave her the letter, and in about ten minutes I felt able to go back to the sitting-room. When I sat down, Samuel said, ''Mima tells me, Priscilla, that thee is very much disappointed about thy letter. I had on this coat when I went to the post-office a week ago, and I didn't put it on again till to-day. I hope thee'll excuse me. Thomas, my son, will thee bring us some red-streaks? I feel as if I could eat a few apples.'

"I felt sorrowful for some time about my sister; but my mind was diverted when we got word that the English Friends were coming to our Monthly Meeting on their way back from Indiana; and as we lived very near the meeting-house, of course they would be at Samuel's. As the time came near, Jemima and I were a good deal interested to have things nice. They were going to be at William Smith's again, where every thing was so neat, and I felt very anxious to make every thing in-doors, at Jemima's, as neat as we could.

"In the sitting-room was one empty corner, where the great rocking-chair ought to stand. It was broken, and put away in the bedroom. I wanted very much to have it mended; but it seemed as if we could not get it to Salem. One time the load would be too large, one time the chair would be forgotten. At last one day it was put in the back of the covered wagon, and fairly started. When Samuel got home it was rather late in the evening, and I heard him say to 'Mima, 'Only think of my forgetting thy large chair. I was late starting from home, thee knows; and when I got to Salem there was a good deal of talk about the war; and when I got half-way home I remembered the big chair in the back of the wagon. It can go in next week.' We did send it again, but it did not get home before Monthly Meeting.

"Jemima had a very neat home-made carpet on the sitting-room: she had a great taste for carpets. As there had been some yards left, she let me cover the front entry too, and her youngest son Edward, a nice lad, helped me put it down. A little colored girl, near by, rubbed up the brass andirons for us, and Edward built up a nice pile of wood ready to kindle the fire when it was wanted. A good many panes of glass had been broken, and as we had just had an equinoctial storm, some old coats, and so on, had been stuffed in at several places; but we managed to get most of the glass put in before Monthly Meeting.

" When we had done all we could to the house, of course we began to think of the cooking. Jemima said, 'I sha'n't be able to get Mary Pearson to come and cook: she is nursing. I wonder whether I hadn't better heat the oven on meeting-day. I can get the dinner in before I go; and then between meetings I can run over and see to it. I shall hardly be missed. I can slip in at the side-door of the meeting-house before Mary Ann has done reading the Minutes.' —'Then thee will heat the oven?' said I.—'I reckon,' she said; 'but it is only a mud oven. Samuel has been talking for a good while about having a brick oven. This one is not very safe.' —'Suppose I make a little sponge-cake, and put it in too,' said I. 'I'll send for some sugar, if thee is willing. Polly Evans used to call me a dabster at sponge-cake.'

" Jemima was willing, and we began to get ready to go to the store. Edward and the little colored girl hunted the barn and the straw-shed, and brought in a quantity of eggs. All could not be sent, because we needed some at home, and some had been set on, and some had lain too long. Then Jemima sent to the garret for brooms and rags, and spared a little butter,—not much, to be sure, when Monthly Meeting was coming. I thought I might as well ride over with Edward; and when we had got coffee, and tea, and so on, and were just starting home, I caught sight of some lemons. I bought a few, and when I got home asked Jemima if she would not like some lemon-puddings. 'Thy apple-pies and rice-puddings are nice, dear,' I said; 'but Hannah Purley and Jonathan are such strangers, we might go a little out of the common way.' Jemima smiled some at my being so anxious, but agreed, as she generally did.

" Fourth-day morning we were up very early. Jemima was going to roast some fowls and a loin of veal. Edward and the little colored girl helped me to beat eggs, grate lemons, and roll sugar; and every thing was ready for the oven before the Friends came in from a distance, who always stopped before meeting to get a cup of tea.

" We had a nice little table for them, of course, —dried beef, preserves, and so on; and one woman Friend, a single woman, asked for a warm flat-iron to press out her cap and hand-kerchief. At last we were ready to start. Jemima had set every thing into the oven, which stood out in the yard. She put the meats back, and the cakes and puddings near the door, where it was not so hot. 'The door isn't very safe,' said she, 'and I propped a stick against it to keep it up. Don't let the dog knock it down, Susan, while we are gone.'

" The day was beautiful; all signs of the storm over, except the roads a little muddy; and as we stepped over to the meeting-house Jemima whispered, 'I am glad I told Susan to set both tables. I think we shall have a good many to dinner. I wanted cole-slaw, like Pennsylvania folks, but the cows broke in last night and ate all the solid cabbage.' She did not talk of these things generally going into meeting; but our minds were very full.

"First Meeting was rather long, for several Friends spoke besides the strangers. When it broke, Jemima stepped out, and I quietly followed her. We walked over to the house, and round into the side-yard, going toward the oven. But just as we had got into the yard we saw the old sow. She had broken out of the barn-yard, and had been wallowing in a pond of brown water near the fence. Now she had knocked down Jemima's stick, and as the door fell I guess she smelt our good things, for she had her fore-feet upon the oven floor. We ran and screamed, but she did not turn. She made a jump up to the oven, over my cakes and puddings, the veal and chickens, and carried the oven roof off with her. Oh, dear! oh, dear!

poor Jemima! I could laugh too, if it wasn't so dreadful."

Reader.—And what did they do then?

Writer.—The best that they could. I do wonder at Jemima, poor thing, to undertake so much on Monthly Meeting day.

.

THE END.

Forgiven at Last. A Novel. By Jeannette R. HADERMANN. 12mo. Fine cloth. $1.75.

" A well-told romance. It is of that order of tales originating with Miss Charlotte Brontë."—*N. Y. Even. Post.*

" The style is animated, and the characters are not deficient in individuality."—*Phila. Age.*

The Old Countess. A Romance. From the German of EDMUND HOFER, by the translator of " Over Yonder," " Magdalena," etc. 12mo. Fine cloth. $1.

"A charming story of life in an old German castle, told in the pleasant German manner that attracts attention and keeps it throughout."—*The Phila. Day.* " The story is not long, is sufficiently involved to compel wonder and suspense, and ends very happily."—*The North American.* " An interesting story."—*The Inquirer.*

Bound Down; or, Life and Its Possibilities. A Novel. By ANNA M. FITCH. 12mo. Fine cloth. $1.50.

"It is a remarkable book."—*N. Y. Even. Mail.* "An interesting domestic story, which will be perused with pleasure from beginning to end."—*Baltimore Even. Bulletin.*

"The author of this book has genius; it is written cleverly, with occasional glimpses into deep truths. . . . Dr. Marston and Mildred are splendid characters."—*Phila. Presbyterian.*

Henry Courtland; or, What A Farmer can Do. A Novel. By A. J. CLINE. 12mo. Fine cloth. $1.75.

" This volume belongs to a class of prose fiction unfortunately as rare as it is valuable. . . . The whole story hangs well together."—*Phila. Press.*

Rougegorge. By Harriet Prescott Spofford. With other Short Stories by ALICE CARY, LUCY H. HOOPER, JANE G. AUSTIN, A. L. WISTER, L. C. DAVIS, FRANK LEE BENEDICT, etc. 8vo. With Frontispiece. Paper cover. 50 cents.

" This is a rare collection."—*Chicago Even. Journal.* " Admirable series of attractive Tales." - *Charleston Courier.*

" The contents are rich, varied and attractive."—*Pittsburg Gazette.*

The Great Empress. An Historical Portrait. By Professor SCHELE DE VERE, of the University of Virginia. 12mo. Extra cloth. $1.75.

" This portrait of Agrippina is drawn with great distinctness, and the book is almost dramatic in its interest."—*N. Y. Observer.*

Nora Brady's Vow, and Mona the Vestal. By

MRS. ANNA H. DORSEY. 12mo. Fine cloth. $1.75.

"These interesting tales describe Ireland and her people in ancient and modern times respectively. 'Mona the Vestal' gives an account of the religious, intellectual, political and social status of the ancient Irish; and 'Nora Brady's Vow' illustrates the devotion and generosity of the Irish women who live in our midst to friends and kindred at home."—*Philada Ledger.*

Helen Erskine. By Mrs. M. Harrison Robinson

12mo. Toned paper. Fine cloth. 1.50.

"There is a varied interest well sustained in this story, and no reader will complain of it as wanting in incident. Higher praise we can give it by saying that the tone is pure and elevated."—*The Age.*

The Quaker Partisans. A Story of the Revolu-

tion. By the author of "The Scout." With Illustrations. 12mo. Extra cloth. $1.50. Paper cover. 60 cents.

"It is a story of stirring incidents turning upon the actual movements of the war, and is told in an animated style of narrative which is very attractive. Its hand- some illustrations will still further recommend it to the young people."—*N. Y. Times.*

One Poor Girl. The Story of Thousands. By

WIRT SIKES. 12mo. Toned paper. Extra cloth. $1.50.

"A deep interest attaches to the volume."—*St. Louis Republican.*
"It is a moving story of a beautiful girl's temptation and trial and triumph, in which appears many an appeal which Christian men and women might well ponder."—*Watchman and Reflector.*

Aspasia. A Tale. By C. Holland. 12mo.

Tinted paper. Extra cloth. $1.25.

"It is a very interesting sketch of a life of vicissitudes, trials, triumphs and wonderful experience. . . . It is well worth reading, and we commend it to extensive circulation."—*St. Louis Democrat.*

The Professor's Wife; or, It Might Have Been.

By ANNIE L. MACGREGOR, author of "John Ward's Governess." 12mo. Fine cloth. $1.75.

"The story is admirably related, without affectation or pretence, and is very touching in parts. Miss Macgregor has great skill in drawing and individualizing character."—*Phila. Press.*

Only a Girl. A Romance. From the German

of Wilhelmine Von Hillern. By MRS. A. L. WISTER, translator of "The Old Mam'selle's Secret," etc. Fourth edition. 12mo. Fine cloth. $2.

"This is a charming work, charmingly written, and no one who reads it can lay it down without feeling impressed with the superior talent of its gifted author. As a work of fiction it will compare favorably in style and interest with the best efforts of the most gifted writers of the day, while in the purity of its tone, and the sound moral lesson it teaches, it is equal, if not superior, to any work of the character that has for years come under our notice."—*Pittsburg Dispatch.*
"Timely, forcible and possessing far more than ordinary merits."—*Phila North American.*

Cottage Piety Exemplified. By the author of

"Union to Christ," "Love to God," etc. 16mo. Extra cloth. $1.25.
"A very interesting sketch."—*N. Y. Observer.*

Stories for Sundays, Illustrating the Catechism.

By the author of "Little Henry and his Bearer." Revised and
edited by A. CLEVELAND COXE, Bishop of Western New York,
and author of "Thoughts on the Services," etc. 12mo. Illustrated. Tinted paper. Extra cloth. $1.75. FINE EDITION.
Printed within red lines. Extra cloth, gilt edges. $2.50.

"We are glad to see this charming book in such a handsome dress. *This* was one of our few Sunday books when we were a school-boy. Sunday books are more plentiful now, but we doubt whether there is any improvement on Mrs. Sherwood's sterling stories for the young."—*Lutheran Observer.*

"The typography is attractive, and the stories illustrated by pictures which render them yet more likely to interest the young people for whose religious improvement they are designed."—*N. Y. Evening Post.*

An Index to the Principal Works in Every De-

partment of Religious Literature. Embracing nearly Seventy
Thousand Citations, Alphabetically Arranged under Two Thou-
sand Heads. By HOWARD MALCOM, D. D., LL.D. SECOND
EDITION. With Addenda to 1870. 8vo. Extra cloth. $4.

"A work of immense labor, such as no one could prepare who had not the years allotted to the lifetime of man. We know of no work of the kind which can compare with it in value."—*Portland Zion's Advocate.*
"The value of such a book can hardly be overestimated. It is a noble contribu-

tion to literature. It meets an urgen need, and long after Dr. Malcom shal have left the world many an earnest penworker will thank him, with heartfelt benedictions on his name, for help and service rendered."—*Boston Watchman and Reflector.*

The Geological Evidences of the Antiquity of Man,

with Remarks on the Origin of Species by Variation. By SIR
CHARLES LYELL, F.R.S., author of "Principles of Geology," etc.
Illustrated by wood-cuts. Second American, from the latest London,
Edition. 8vo. Extra cloth. $3.

This work treats of one of the most interesting scientific subjects of the day, and will be examined with interest, as well by

those who favor its deductions as by those who condemn them.

The Student's Manual of Oriental History. A

Manual of the Ancient History of the East, to the Commencement
of the Median Wars. By FRANCOIS LENORMANT, Sub-Librarian
of the Imperial Institute of France, and E. CHEVALLIER, Member of
the Royal Asiatic Society, London. 2 vols. 12mo. Fine cloth. $5.50.

"The best proof of the immense results accomplished in the various departments of philology is to be found in M.

Francois Lenormant's admirable *Handbook of Ancient History.*"—*London Athenæum.*

GOOD BOOKS FOR YOUNG READERS.

Deep Down. A Tale of the Cornish Mines. By R. M. BALLANTYNE, author of "Fighting the Flames," "Silver Lake," etc. With Illustrations. Globe edition. 12mo. Fine cloth. $1.50.

"'Deep Down' can be recommended as a story of exciting interest, which boys will eagerly read, and which will give some valuable ideas on a subject about which very little is generally known. The book is embellished with a number of very excellent designs."—*Philada. Even. Telegraph.*

Fighting the Flames. A Tale of the Fire Brigade. By R. M. BALLANTYNE, author of "Silver Lake," "The Coral Islands," etc. With Illustrations. Globe edition. 12mo. Fine cloth. $1.50.

"An interesting and spirited little work."—*Philada. Even. Telegraph.*

Erling the Bold. A Tale of the Norse Sea-Kings. By R. M. BALLANTYNE, author of "Fighting the Flames," "Deep Down," etc. Globe edition. With Illustrations. 12mo. Extra cloth. $1.50.

"It is a bold and stirring tale of the old Norse rovers who conquered and settled in England at various times between the fifth and eleventh centuries. The narrative is interesting of itself, and it gives an excellent description of the manners and customs of the rugged race who inhabited the North of Europe at the dawn of modern history."—*Philada. Telegraph.*

Silver Lake; or, Lost in the Snow. By R. M. BALLANTYNE, author of "The Wild Man of the West," "Fighting the Flames," etc. With Illustrations. Square 12mo. Tinted paper. Extra cloth. $1.25.

"We heartily recommend the book, and can imagine the pleasure many a young heart will receive on its perusal."—*The Eclectic Review.*

Forty-Four Years of a Hunter's Life. Being Reminiscences of Meshach Browning, a Maryland Hunter. With numerous Illustrations. Globe edition. 12mo. Fine cloth. $1.50.

"It portrays the mode of life of the early settlers, the dangers they encountered, and all the difficulties they had to contend with, and how successfully a strong arm and a courageous heart could overcome them. It is a book which will be read with the greatest avidity by thousands in all sections of the country."—*Balt. American.*

Moody Mike; or, The Power of Love. A Christmas Story. By FRANK SEWALL. Illustrated. 16mo. Extra cloth. $1.

This is a story intended for the young folks. It is published in a manner at once neat and attractive, being well printed and beautifully bound. It is also illustrated with several full-page engravings, which impart to it additional attractions.

GOOD BOOKS FOR YOUNG READERS.

Man Upon the Sea; or, A History of Maritime

Adventure, Exploration and Discovery from the Earliest Ages to the Present Time. With numerous Engravings. By FRANK B. GOODRICH, author of "The Court of Napoleon," etc. 8vo. Cloth. $2.25.

"It is a delightful work, brilliant with deeds of valiant enterprise and heroic endurance, and varied by every conceivable incident. We have seldom seen a work more agreeable in style or more fascinating in interest."—*Boston Journal.*

"The book will be warmly welcomed by young people."—*Boston Post.*

Old Deccan Days; or, Hindoo Fairy Legends

Current in Southern India. Collected from oral tradition by M. FRERE. With an Introduction and Notes by Sir Bartle Frere. Globe edition. 12mo. Illustrated. Fine cloth. $1.50.

"This little collection of Hindoo Fairy Legends is probably the most interesting book extant on that subject. . . . The stories of this little book are told in a very lively and agreeable style—a style few writers of English possess, but which, when it belongs to a lady, is the best and most attractive in the world."—*N. Y. Times.*

Fuz-Buz and Mother Grabem. The Wonderful

Stories of Fuz-Buz the Fly and Mother Grabem the Spider. A Fairy Tale. Handsomely Illustrated. Small 4to. Cloth. $1. Extra cloth, gilt top. $1.25.

"Laughable stories comically illustrated for little folks. The very book to delight little boys and girls. Get it for the holidays."—*Pittsburg Chronicle.*

Casella; or, The Children of the Valleys. By

MARTHA FARQUHARSON, author of "Elsie Dinsmore," etc. 16mo. Cloth. $1.50.

"It is rich in all that is strong, generous and true."—*Balt. Episc. Methodist.*
"The story is one of the most interesting in ecclesiastical history."—*The Methodist.*

"A lively and interesting story, based upon the sufferings of the pious Waldenses, and is well written and life-like."—*Boston Christian Era.*

Trees, Plants and Flowers: Where and How

they Grow. By WILLIAM L. BAILY, author of "Our Own Birds," etc. With seventy-three Engravings. 16mo. Toned paper. Extra cloth. $1.

"In the compass of less than a hundred and fifty pages Mr. Baily gives us 'a familiar history of the vegetable kingdom,' popularly and interestingly written, well arranged, and containing much valuable information and many interesting facts. He is entitled to great thanks for the work he is doing in aiding the development of a taste for and interest in natural history. We should be glad to see this book generally in the hands of the little folks; it is written so clearly and pleasantly that they will take to it readily. But there are many grown folks also who would be glad to know something more of botany than they do, but who have neither time nor inclination for ponderous technical and scientific volumes. To these also we can heartily commend Mr. Baily's book."—*N. Y. Even. Mail.*

The Old Mam'selle's Secret. *After the German*

of E. Marlitt, author of "Gold Elsie," "Countess Gisela," &c. By MRS. A. L. WISTER. Sixth edition. 12mo. Cloth, $1.75.

"A more charming story, and one which, having once commenced, it seemed more difficult to leave, we have not met with for many a day."—*The Round Table.*

"Is one of the most intense, concentrated, compact novels of the day. . . . And the work has the minute fidelity of the author

of 'The Initials,' the dramatic unity of Reade, and the graphic power of George Elliot."—*Columbus (O.) Journal.*

"Appears to be one of the most interesting stories that we have had from Europe for many a day."—*Boston Traveler.*

Gold Elsie. *From the German of E. Marlitt*,

author of the "Old Mam'selle's Secret," "Countess Gisela," &c. By MRS. A. L. WISTER. Fifth edition. 12mo. Cloth, $1.75.

"A charming book. It absorbs your attention from the title-page to the end."—*The Home Circle.*

"A charming story charmingly told."—*Baltimore Gazette.*

Countess Gisela. *From the German of E. Mar-*

litt, author of "The Old Mam'selle's Secret," "Gold Elsie," "Over Yonder," &c. By MRS. A. L. WISTER. Third Edition. 12mo. Cloth, $1.75.

"There is more dramatic power in this than in any of the stories by the same author that we have read."—*N.O. Times.*

"It is a story that arouses the interest

of the reader from the outset."—*Pittsburg Gazette.*

"The best work by this author."—*Philada. Telegraph.*

Over Yonder. *From the German of E. Marlitt*,

author of "Countess Gisela," "Gold Elsie," &c. Third edition. With a full-page Illustration. 8vo. Paper cover, 30 cts.

"'Over Yonder' is a charming novelette. The admirers of 'Old Mam'selle's Secret' will give it a glad reception, while those who are ignorant of the merits of

this author will find in it a pleasant introduction to the works of a gifted writer."—*Daily Sentinel.*

Three Thousand Miles through th Rocky Moun-

tains. By A. K. McCLURE. Illustrated. 12mo. Tinted paper Extra cloth, $2.

"Those wishing to post themselves on the subject of that magnificent and extraordinary Rocky Mountain dominion should read the Colonel's book."—*New York Times.*

"The work makes one of the most satisfactory itineraries that has been given to us from this region, and must be read with both pleasure and profit."—*Philada. North American.*

"We have never seen a book of Western travels which so thoroughly and completely satisfied us as his. nor one written in such

agreeable and charming style."—*Bradford Reporter.*

"The letters contain many incidents of Indian life and adventures of travel which impart novel charms to them."—*Chicago Evening Journal.*

"The book is full of useful information."—*New York Independent.*

Let him who would have some proper conception of the limitless material richness of the Rocky Mountain region, read this book."—*Charleston (S. C.) Courier.*

Our Own Birds of the United States. A Familiar

Natural History of the Birds of the United States. By WILLIAM L. BAILY. Revised and Edited by Edward D. Cope, Member of the Academy of Natural Sciences. With numerous Illustrations. 16mo. Toned paper. Extra cloth, $1.50.

"The text is all the more acceptable to the general reader because the birds are called by their popular names, and not by the scientific titles of the cyclopædias, and we know them at once as old friends and companions. We commend this unpretending little book to the public as possessing an interest wider in its range but similar in kind to that which belongs to Gilbert White's Natural History of Selborne."—*N. Y. Even. Post.*

"The whole book is attractive, supplying much pleasantly-conveyed information for young readers, and embodying an arrangement and system that will often make it a helpful work of reference for older naturalists."—*Philada. Even. Bulletin.*

"To the youthful, 'Our Own Birds' is likely to prove a bountiful source of pleasure, and cannot fail to make them thoroughly acquainted with the birds of the United States. As a science there is none more agreeable to study than ornithology. We therefore feel no hesitation in commending this book to the public. It is neatly printed and bound, and is profusely illustrated."—*New York Herald.*

A Few Friends, and How They Amused Them-

selves. A Tale in Nine Chapters, containing descriptions of Twenty Pastimes and Games, and a Fancy-Dress Party. By M. E. DODGE, author of "Hans Brinker," &c. 12mo. Toned paper. Extra cloth, $1.25.

"This convenient little encyclopædia strikes the proper moment most fitly. The evenings have lengthened, and until they again become short parties will be gathered everywhere and social intercourse will be general. But though it is comparatively easy to assemble those who would be amused, the amusement is sometimes replaced by its opposite, and more resembles a religious meeting than the juicy entertainment intended. The 'Few Friends' describes some twenty pastimes, all more

or less intellectual, all provident of mirth, requiring no preparation, and capable of enlisting the largest or passing off with the smallest numbers. The description is conveyed by examples that are themselves 'as good as a play.' The book deserves a wide circulation, as it is the missionary of much social pleasure, and demands no more costly apparatus than ready wit and genial disposition." — *Philada. North American.*

Cameos from English History. By the author of

"The Heir of Redclyffe," &c. With marginal Index. 12mo. Tinted paper. Cloth, $1.25; extra cloth, $1.75.

"History is presented in a very attractive and interesting form for young folks in this work."—*Pittsburg Gazette.*

"An excellent design happily executed." —*N.Y. Times.*

The Diamond Edition of the Poetical Works of

Robert Burns. Edited by REV. R. A. WILLMOTT. New edition. With numerous additions. 18mo. Tinted paper. Fine cloth, $1.

"This small, square, compact volume is printed in clear type, and contains, in three hundred pages, the whole of Burns' poems, with a glossary and index. It is cheap,

elegant and convenient, bringing the works of one of the most popular of British poets within the means of every reader."—*Boston Even. Transcript.*

THE

WORKS OF WASHINGTON IRVING.

EDITIONS OF IRVING'S WORKS.

I. The Knickerbocker Edition.—Large 12mo, *on* superfine laid, tinted paper. Profusely Illustrated with Steel Plates and Wood-cuts, elegantly printed from new stereotype plates. Complete in 27 vols. Bound in extra cloth, gilt top. Per vol. $2.50. Half calf, gilt extra. Per vol. $4.

*II. The Riverside Edition.—*16mo, *on fine white* paper; from new stereotype plates. With Steel Plates. Complete in 26 vols. Green crape cloth, gilt top, beveled edges. Per vol. $1.75. Half calf, gilt extra. Per vol. $3.25.

*III. The People's Edition.—From the same stereo-*type plates as above, but printed on cheaper paper. Complete in 26 vols. 16mo. With Steel Vignette Titles. Neatly bound in cloth. Per vol. $1.25. Half calf neat. Per vol. $2.50.

*IV. The Sunnyside Edition.—*12mo, *on fine toned* paper. With Steel Plates. Complete in 28 vols. Handsomely bound in dark-green cloth. Per vol. $2.25. Half calf, gilt extra. Per vol. $4.

Embracing the following :

Bracebridge Hall,	Goldsmith,	Granada,
Wolfert's Roost.	Alhambra,	Salmagundi,
Sketch Book,	Columbus, 3 vols.,	Spanish Papers, 2 vols.
Traveler,	Astoria,	Washington, 5 vols.,
Knickerbocker,	Bonneville,	Life and Letters, 4 vols.
Crayon Miscellany,	Mahomet, 2 vols.,	

The reissue of these works in their several forms is unusually elegant. The plates are new, the paper superior, the printing handsome, and each, in proportion to price, combining good taste with economy.

EACH WORK SOLD SEPARATELY.

www.ingramcontent.com/pod-product-compliance
Lightning Source LLC
Chambersburg PA
CBHW020608030726
47497CB00007B/2131